BEAST'S SECRET BABY

INTERSTELLAR BRIDES® PROGRAM: THE BEASTS

BOOK 7

GRACE GOODWIN

SUBSCRIBE TODAY!

PATREON

*H*i there! Grace Goodwin here. I am SO excited to invite you into my intense, crazy, sexy, romantic, imagination and the worlds born as a result. From Battlegroup Karter to The Colony and on behalf of the entire Coalition Fleet of Planets, I welcome you! Visit my Patreon page for additional bonus content, sneak peaks, and insider information on upcoming books as well as the opportunity to receive NEW RELEASE BOOKS before anyone else! See you there! ~ Grace

Grace's PATREON: https://www.patreon.com/gracegoodwin

FIND YOUR INTERSTELLAR MATCH!

YOUR mate is out there. Take the test today and discover your perfect match. Are you ready for a sexy alien mate (or two)?

VOLUNTEER NOW!
interstellarbridesprogram.com

1

Atlan Warlord Velik, Key Biscayne, Florida

HOW LONG HAD I been running on this beach? Wet sand sank beneath my feet and clung to my skin like tiny parasites. Within me, the beast raged.

Not long enough.

The beast craved violence. Demanded to be set free, to rip the head from every human on the planet as punishment for a crime they had not committed.

Hide mate.

Gods be damned. Not this again. "No one is hiding our mate."

Hide mate. Kill all. Find her.

Fuck. Killing a bunch of humans was not going to help me find a mate. We'd had this argument before, many times.

Until recently, I'd been winning the test of wills with my beast. Now, as the mating fever grew ever stronger, my control was rapidly slipping away. I'd been tempted to give in, more than once. To release the rage and pain of not finding her. Our mate. We both needed her. Now. Right fucking now.

Kill. Make them pay.

"They aren't hiding her. Now shut the fuck up." I shouted the last and a group of sunbathing visitors turned, their slathering of sunblock, towel shaking, umbrella planting activities paused, midmotion, to stare at me. No doubt due to the volume of my voice...and my size.

Every tourist, beach comber, lifeguard, and child I ran past gaped, eyes rounded, some taking multiple steps away as I neared. All except one small human child who held up a bright yellow shovel smaller than my hand and waited for me to help stack piles of wet sand into some kind of structure.

Most I ignored. The little one I thanked for the offer before moving on. And on. And on.

That had been when the sun was high. Now it dipped close to the horizon, glowing behind the human city I'd been assigned to these long months, time during which I had hoped to find her. My mate. The only being in the universe who could save me. I did my job, guarded the Coalition's processing center as they accepted new brides and fighters. I also helped my fellow Atlans when I could, but I'd never been at home here, amidst the stares and, at times, hostility.

Alien. Outcast. I was from another world and most of the small-minded humans refused to look beyond that.

I was larger than a human. This was not news. Seeing a beast such as Braun or Tane on their small television screens in the ridiculous matchmaking program was much different than seeing an Atlan male, in the flesh, shouting at nothing, I supposed. Shouting at no one. At himself.

I am beast. Not no one.

"I know."

I fight. I kill. I hunt. I protect. I serve. Reward. Want mate now.

"I know. I am looking for her. Every day." The words came out in short bursts as my feet hit the sand. I ran barefoot along the edge of the water. My shorts were soaked through from a combination of salt water and sweat. I'd taken my shirt off hours ago, the heat of the sun on my skin soothing.

At least the sun shined upon me with warmth.

Hurt them. Make them tell us.

The beast forced me to look at a group of young humans playing a game with a white ball and a tall net. It appeared the challenge was to get the ball back over the top of the net before it touched ground.

Young males strutted and made jests as they competed for the attention and affection of the scantily clad females. Their bodies were on display, both sexes. Meant to entice a mate.

I looked at each of the females in turn as I approached, then ran past. Smooth, round breasts. Soft skin. Long, shapely legs. They were beautiful females, every one of them. In my youth, I would have taken any of them to my bed for hours of pleasure. Now, my beast demanded only one female. Would accept just one. Our mate. I looked at the perfect, fragile females. Inspected their bodies. Their curves should have made my cock instantly hard. I should have wanted to touch, to taste, to explore.

I felt nothing.

No. Not mine.

"No shit, Sherlock." I'd picked up the human expression from one of the human fighters who had come through the center. I had asked him what it meant. Apparently, this Sherlock was a brilliant human investigator and solver of crimes. I had no idea if this were true, but the expression stuck.

I am Velik. Not Sherlock. I kill Sherlock.

My beast had zero sense of humor.

Earth was not so different from Atlan. Slightly different colors. Different culture. But beautiful, just as home had been.

A home I hadn't seen in two decades.

Overheated from my run, I turned and ran straight out into the water. The waves pushed at me. Even the beast realized the water in this bay was stronger than he was. Relentless. It could drag us under and kill us both with zero effort.

Not a lot of things could do so.

The smell of salt water and fish had become easy to ignore. The cool water calmed my body and slowed my heartbeat even as my thoughts raced. I had avoided this action for as long as I could. I had no honorable choices left to me.

The beast grumbling with disagreement, I activated the embedded comm Dr. Helion had implanted behind my ear years ago. When I left the Intelligence Core and asked to be assigned to Earth, I'd sworn I would never talk to him again.

The only reason anyone ever spoke to Helion was to give a report, get a new assignment, or they were ready to die. When I left the I.C., I'd had none of those reasons. My plan? To guard the Coalition Fleet's processing center and—I had hoped—find a human bride. I'd been here for several years, looking, waiting. The beast gained power and control daily. I could not afford to wait another day.

"Warlord Velik, this is a surprise." Helion's voice was calm and calculating, as always. When serving under his command, that steady confidence provided the calm in the storm. If Helion gave an order, we all knew the decision had been made with ice cold, unbiased analysis.

"Commander." The waves pushed at my chest, the crashing sound loud to my ears. I knew the comm would filter out everything but my voice.

"Is your Mating Fever truly so severe?"

Of course he would know what I wanted. Why else would I contact him? I closed my eyes and surrendered to my fate. "I am too far gone to return to Atlan. I need an assignment. A mission. I'm done."

"Are you sure about this? Once I set the plan into motion, there will be no second chance."

Something bit my leg. I ignored the slight annoyance. As I spoke, the same stinging sensation occurred several more times on both legs. Perhaps this was the gods' way of helping me focus as I asked Helion to help me die with honor. "I cannot hold out any longer. I have failed to find a mate here. I would end my suffering serving the Coalition rather than rotting in a prison cell on Atlan."

"Very well. How long?"

The beast fought to transform, to be free. Fought hard. "The sooner the better. I don't think I'll last a week."

"Fuck." I heard true regret in Helion's voice. Perhaps the male did have a soul. "I need that week, Velik. I will get you out of there sooner if I can."

"Thank you." The relief made my legs crumble beneath me and I rode the next set of waves to the shore.

"Just a moment. I need to ping your transport beacon."

I sat in the sand, staring at nothing as I waited. The

transport beacon surgically implanted near my hip buzzed my flesh with an all-too-familiar sensation.

"Contact confirmed." Helion sighed. "All right, Warlord. Hang on as long as you can. I will get you out of there."

The comm link went dead and I laid back on the sand. Hands under my head, I watched puffy white clouds move across the sky for long minutes. Until the beast startled to attention.

I was on my feet before I realized a battle for control of my body had even begun.

Mate. Mine.

What the fuck was he—

Then I heard a voice—*her* voice. I turned to look out over the waves to discover a boat with sails moving across the water a hundred yards offshore. The craft was not overly large, and I counted no more than a dozen humans lounging about while three other humans adjusted the ropes and sails. Gusts of wind blew into my face from the southeast. My beast growled.

His senses were even more astute than mine, but we *both* smelled her.

Fuck. My cock instantly hardened. Already addicted. I breathed deeply, memorizing the scent of cherry blossoms and a sweet spice I was not familiar with. There were no cherry trees here. Perhaps the scent came from the soap she chose when she bathed...

Images of thrusting deep inside our female while holding her up against the wall of a shower flooded my mind as my beast took off sprinting down the beach.

Fuck me, we were chasing a sailboat. The irritation on my legs increased, but nothing would deter the beast from following our mate. Nothing. If I wanted even a semblance of control, I had to give in and run. Hard. Fast.

The beast had her scent. He would hunt. There were multiple females sitting on the boat. We did not know which one was our mate. Which female belonged to us was not important, only the fact that she existed, we had found her, and we would die before we let her go.

2

*S*tefani Davis, Biscayne Bay, Florida

I LEANED BACK, bracing my weight on stiff upper arms as the sailboat cut through the waves. At least once a month I made time, with my friends Carmen and Henry, to spend an afternoon on the water. Now that both my mom and my twin sister had mated Atlan Warlords, and my mother had actually moved to another planet, I spent a lot of time alone. Too much time.

A twin without their twin was a sad, pathetic thing. Out on the water was the only time I felt alive anymore. And free.

Lifting my face to the sun, I let out a loud whoop. "I love sailing!"

Sitting right next to me on the bow of the forty-footer, Carmen laughed. "Me, too."

Henry handed us both another margarita and settled on a folded towel next to Carmen as the sail snapped and waves crashed around us. "And this, lovely ladies, is why you will never convince me to leave Florida."

I was about to agree when Carmen smacked my leg. Hard. "Effing-A Stef. Look at that guy on the beach. Total hunk."

I turned my head to follow her gaze and almost dropped the frozen margarita in my lap.

Oh, god! Oh shit! That was an Atlan! Had to be. He was too big, too gorgeous with his shirt off. Jeez, he was showing too much...muscle. "He should put on a shirt."

"Are you insane?" Carmen leaned forward and pulled a pair of small binoculars from where they rested around her neck. She lifted them so she could spy on the man. "What is *wrong* with you? He's way too hot to cover up."

With a knowing grin, I met Henry's gaze. Henry grinned like he always did when he was feeling the effects of the marijuana gummies his cousin shipped to him every couple of months. Illegal here? Totally. Did Henry care? No.

I didn't mind. I'd grown up too poor, around too much suffering, to bother with judging how other people coped. Despite Henry's weekend vice, we both knew Carmen was the real wild woman. Henry nudged her with his shoulder. "You going to try to find him when we get back to shore? We're getting close."

I checked my watch and sighed. He was right. About ten minutes and we'd be walking off the boat. Damn it.

"He's running." Carmen giggled. "Oh my god. Stef, I think that guy is chasing the boat."

"What?"

Carmen handed me her binoculars and I looked for myself.

I shouldn't have looked. Now my peaceful day on the

water was instantly ruined by a throbbing, horny vajayjay influenced by a bit too much tequila.

Seriously? Could this guy be any more perfect? He moved like he could run at top speed for hours. He wasn't even breathing hard. The sun made his skin glow, from sweat or the water splashing beneath his feet, I wasn't sure. Didn't matter. All it did was define every muscle in his chest and across his back. His thighs and legs stretched and contracted as he ran, every muscle popping out to say hello. His shorts were thin and did nothing to hide his bouncing... Holy shit. He was *huge*! What would that feel like all up in my business? Was that what my sister rode every chance she got? And my *mother*?

Not going there. Not. Going. There. Eyes up, Stefani.

His dark hair was just long enough to flow back from a face that looked carved from granite. Definitely an Atlan. But they were based in Miami, near the Interstellar Brides Processing center. As far as I knew, Miami was the only city in the country that had agreed to allow aliens—and not the green card kind, the outer space kind—to take up permanent residence in the country. And this was *not* Miami. We were miles and miles from Miami. "What the hell is he doing all the way out here?"

Carmen grabbed the binoculars from my hands and held them up to ogle him again. "Who cares why he's here. He is perfect."

"No, he's not." He was an alien and breaking a few dozen new laws right now. I didn't want to get him into trouble, but he really needed to turn that toned ass around and start running back the way he'd come.

"You know him?" she asked.

"Not exactly. But I know guys like him." More than one, as a matter of fact. I didn't simply *know* the Atlan warlords

Max and Kovo. Technically, thanks to my mother and my twin taking them as mates, those two huge mountains of alien man-meat were family.

"Come on, Stef. You don't even know him and you're judging him? Why? Because he's too fuckable?" Carmen's voice had gone husky, as if she was already in bed with him in her imagination.

Henry nearly choked, his burst of laughter shooting a mouthful of margarita onto the deck of the boat. "Carmen, you are shameless."

"Hell yeah, when it comes to what I want. You two should be more like me. You'd have a lot more fun."

I watched the Atlan run for long moments. He was lickable, for sure. Did my repressed sex drive want to climb him like a tree and not stop until I passed out from orgasmic exhaustion? Oh, yes, she did. But sex with an Atlan was not fun. Dangerous? Extremely. "I'm fine. I don't need any more fun in my life."

Fun, to Carmen, was clubs, parties, drinking and taking a hot new man home for a night of sweaty sex. Sometimes she kept them for a few weeks. Sometimes she kicked them out of bed before she fell asleep. I wasn't sure what she was looking for in a partner, or if she was looking for anything permanent at all. She seemed to be enjoying herself, so more power to her. I, however, had zero interest in making my life any more complicated than it already was. Two alien family members, a mother on another planet, a twin who was too busy having orgasms to remember to call me, two jobs—because I refused to accept another dime of Max's money—because taking his money made me feel like my mother was a prostitute —and a college degree to finish. The Warlord Maxus scholarship that covered tuition? Okay. The *I'm-out-of toilet-paper-and-groceries* fund? No.

Carmen turned away from the hottie on the beach to stare at me. "Stef, you are so serious all the time. He's gorgeous. You should ask Adrian to hook you up with one of those beasts like on TV. Set you up on a date with one of those guys."

"I do not want a relationship right now."

She laughed. "Who said anything about a relationship? All I'm saying is I wouldn't kick any of them out of bed." She practically purred the word bed as I blinked away my surprise that she'd recognized him for what he was. Atlan. A beast.

I sighed. I'd met enough Atlans to know one when I saw one. I'd spent several weeks on their planet after my mother found herself mated to one. I was happy for her, and Warlord Maxus was great—more than great—but that did *not* mean I wanted a big, growling, bossy warlord for myself.

My twin sister, Adrian, had done me dirty and hooked up with an Atlan while we were visiting mom and Maxus. Adrian and her new mate, Kovo, came back to Earth to live. To say my sister was obsessed with her new man was an understatement. It was like he'd drugged her with orgasms, and she'd never recovered. Warlord Kovo, my new brother-in-law, was good to her. He treated her like a queen, so I could hardly complain. I was thrilled that she'd found someone who would love her the way she deserved. My twin was the best human on the planet. If Kovo ever broke her heart, I would kill him—even if I had to hire an entire squadron of Special Ops snipers to do it.

I'd pondered how to murder him many times—just in case. I wasn't sure even a SWAT team would be enough to take one of these warlords down. They were too strong. Too big. Too...much.

I missed spending time with my twin, but true love,

especially in the whole 'honeymoon' phase, tended to make people a little crazy. Adrian and Kovo were way more than a *little* crazy for each other.

And with a cock like that? No wonder...

Shut up and stop thinking about my brother-in-law's junk, that's what I was going to do. I didn't want to be irrational and foolish like my sister. Obsession? No thanks. I wanted my head on straight and my feet on the ground, thank you very much. No kids. No husband. No freaking Golden Retriever named Rosie or a stupid lawn that needed to be weeded and mowed every weekend. Three bedroom house with toilets to clean and dog shit to pick up in the back yard? *Hell* no.

Henry took the binoculars from Carmen. "You mean he's one of those aliens, like on that bachelor TV show? What do they call them?"

"Atlan Warlords."

A long, slow whistle left Henry's lips. "Fuck me, that guy is ripped. How are the rest of us supposed to compete with that?" Henry whistled again, louder this time and the Atlan turned his head in our direction. "Ripped, and fast."

"I told you; he's following us." Carmen sipped at her margarita and stared at the Atlan as he picked up speed. "Stef, I swear he really is chasing the boat. Why would he do that?"

"I don't know." I didn't. Not for sure. Carmen was right, it did *look* like he was pacing the boat, keeping us in sight. Then again, maybe he was training for a marathon. Or blowing off steam. Or just trying to keep that freaking fabulous body in tip-top shape.

If he was tracking our boat? Well, shit. That could only mean one thing—he thought his mate was on this sailboat. We were going to hit the docks and an eight foot tall alien was going to walk up to one of the handful of women on our boat—mostly tourists—and say the one word that would start all kinds of trouble...*mine.*

A few minutes later, everyone was watching him run. The closer we got to shore, the more they paid attention. Even the crew members were talking about him, wondering what the massive football or hockey player was doing running after the boat. They speculated that he was a new recruit for one of the local professional sports teams. Why Miami even had a hockey team—duh, it's *hot* here—was beyond me.

We all watched. He ran. The theories about him continued.

Carmen, Henry, and I remained silent. We knew he was no such thing. He wasn't an Olympic bodybuilder, or a professional wrestler. He didn't play basketball. He was an alien, and he didn't give a shit about football or any other human sport. The best I could judge, based on Maxus and Kovo, warlords only cared about two things. Fighting and fucking, and not necessarily in that order.

I lost sight of him when our boat drifted past a group of pilings and floated toward the pier. The sails were down and our tour guides used an inboard motor to move us into place at the dock. One of the crew hopped off to tie the lines as another dropped the fenders. I'd watched this process at least a dozen times and still sighed in disappointment. Fun over. Now I would have to save enough money for the next time.

As the passengers began to disembark, I threw my white cotton shirt on over my hot pink bikini top, and wiggled into the cute swim skirt that came with the set. I loved a sexy, barely-there, G-string bikini bottom as much as the next girl, but only when I was on the beach or at the pool. I didn't walk around the docks with my ass hanging out. I had *some* standards.

My sandals were a bit sturdier than flip-slops. Velcro closures covered with sparkling golden glitter crisscrossed the tops of my feet. My new pedicure had turned my toenails a bright, happy, sunshine yellow that matched my beach towel. I was, after all, trying to cheer myself up.

Carmen, Henry and I always sat near the front of the boat, which meant we were in the back of the line waiting to get off. I slung my beach bag over my shoulder and waited. I'd packed it full of sunscreen, a towel and a few other odds and ends. I was watching one of the crew members assist an elderly gentleman onto the pier when Henry nudged me. "I don't believe it. There's that alien. He actually caught up."

"Where?" Carmen's head swiveled like she was a bobble-head toy. Her dark brown eyes had grown big and round like an owl's. "He's so hot. I hope he's here for me." She giggled. "I tried out for that Bachelor Beast show, you know. I auditioned twice."

"You did not," I said.

"Oh, yes, I did." She rubbed her hands together. "They're going to have auditions for the next season soon. Third time's a charm, right?" She glanced up at me, then back down the pier, trying to spot the alien. "I'm not kidding, Stef. I want one."

"Are you crazy?" I shook my head as I handed the remains of my margarita to one of the crewmembers, along with a hefty tip. I was coming back, I wanted them to remember me and give me my preferred spot on the boat next time, right at the front where the wind hit my face and the waves splashed on either side of me. The extra cash had worked so far. In fact, the last two times I'd walked onto the boat they'd greeted me by name.

"What do you mean, am I crazy? What's wrong with you? He's gorgeous. And if he's one of those aliens, he will be totally devoted and loyal and..." Carmen shivered. "Horny. Did you even watch the show? The first season? He grabbed that makeup girl and claimed her up against the dressing room door with the cameras rolling in the hall. She was enjoying herself, everyone watching could hear them going at it like animals."

Yes, I had watched the show. No, I did not want to be claimed—aka fucked—by an Atlan beast on live television.

Carmen's attention was focused beyond me, somewhere down the pier. "He's a dream come true, if you ask me."

"You can have him." I wanted no part of that kind of obsessive, smothering, controlling relationship. Henry chuckled at my muttering.

"If I were gay, I'd be all over that. I agree with Carmen."

I laughed. "Well, maybe he's into tag teams and you two can share him."

Shifting my weight as I stepped from the boat to the pier, I looked up just as the alien in question turned the final corner in the maze of wooden planks and walkways. He had tracked the boat to our section of the pier and walked straight toward our boat.

Toward me.

His gazed locked with mine.

Oh, shit.

I froze.

Carmen bumped into me from behind. "What? Sorry, I—"

Henry bumped into her, making us a threesome of dominos about to tip over onto the pier. I heard Henry curse under his breath, then catch himself. "Are you okay? I didn't mean to step on—" The words died in his throat. "Whoa."

Okay then. I wasn't hallucinating. Henry saw him, too.

"Stef?" Carmen whispered my name over my shoulder.

"Yes?"

"I think he's staring at you."

Forcing my feet to *move*, I pretended the warlord *wasn't* looking at me and walked forward, toward him. Carmen and Henry followed close behind. None of us said a word and I congratulated myself on my feigned nonchalance.

A few more steps and we would be walking past him, leaving him behind us. He would be a memory; that really hot guy we saw running on the beach that one day.

"Stop." The deep, rumbling voice went straight to my core and made my vajayjay squirm. If she could talk, she would be screaming at him to fill her up and—

"Excuse me?" Unable to avoid looking directly at him for a moment longer, I lifted my head and looked him in the eye.

Mistake. Huge mistake. There was lust in his eyes. Need. Obsession. None of which I wanted. However, my damn vajayjay went wet and achy and invited him over. I saw the moment the scent of my arousal hit him. He shuddered and closed his eyes like he'd just taken a hit of the best drug ever.

"Mine."

Oh, shit. There it was.

"No, Warlord. I'm sorry. I am not yours." I shrugged and nodded my head back over my shoulder. "Maybe you were talking to Carmen?"

Carmen peeked around my shoulder. She was a couple inches shorter than me, her gorgeous tawny skin had bright coral accents where she'd received a bit too much sun on her cheeks. Her curly black hair was pulled back to reveal a bone structure that could belong to a magical pixie. Her natural beauty a look I had envied more times than I could count.

"Hi. I'm Carmen." The invitation was there, in her eyes. No mistaking that come-and-get-me look.

The Atlan glanced at her for less than a second before returning his intense stare to me. "Name."

Was that a question?

"Stefani, but we call her Stef."

I groaned. "Thanks, Carmen."

"Anytime." She sounded so smug I was tempted to turn around and give her the finger, but I didn't dare take my eyes off the warlord in front of me. My instincts insisted if I turned away, I would end up thrown over his shoulder.

"Stefani. Mine." His voice had dropped at least half an octave. I watched as he shuddered again. He was huge, like all the Atlans I'd met. His veins bulged from his temples. I refused to look lower.

Would. Not. Look—

Holy hell. His shorts hid nothing. His cock was huge, and hard and straining toward me through the thin material of his shorts.

No. No. No.

Lower. Look lower. Legs. Legs were safe, right?

"What the hell happened to your legs?" The words burst from my lips before I could censor them.

"Mine."

One track freaking mind. I held up my hand, palm out, as I crouched down to get a better look at his legs. He was covered in jellyfish stings. Covered. That had to hurt. A lot.

"Jesus, man. What did you do? Put on jelly perfume and invite them over?" Henry whistled and stepped up next to me, completely ignoring the massive alien who could crush his skull with one hand.

I looked up at the Atlan to find him watching me, his dark eyes focused on me like the rest of the world didn't exist. I had to admit, it was nice. No surprise there. I'd seen Kovo give my sister the same look. She melted like butter every time. "What's your name, Warlord?"

"Velik."

"You from the processing center?"

"Yes."

"One of the guards? I think I remember one of the guys mentioning you."

"Yes."

I wracked my brain. I knew I'd heard his name. Knew it. "Wait! You're the one who helped Maxus get the mating cuffs!" Maxus had been on Earth illegally and had to request a pair of smuggled mating cuffs be sent to Earth so he could slap them on my mother's wrists.

"Yes." His dinner-plate sized hands were now clenched into fists at his sides. How bad was his mating fever? How close was he to losing control and letting his beast out? If that happened, there would be nothing I could do, no way to get him back where he belonged before he made a huge mistake. "Stefani. Mine."

"We'll talk about that later." He did seem determined. I didn't want a mate, but I couldn't just stand here and let him suffer. He had at least a dozen stings as well as visible tentacles still sticking to his legs. I swung my bag around and dug through it looking for my bottle of *Sting Stopper*. "Found it!"

I pulled the treatment spray from my bag and shook the bottle. It was nearly empty. I couldn't even get the sprayer to work. "Mine's gone. Either one of you have any?"

Carmen shook her head. "No. Sorry."

Henry shrugged. "No. And I'm not peeing on his legs."

Carmen burst out laughing. The Atlan growled in warning and took a step toward Henry.

Moving quickly, I stepped between them and held up my hand. Mistake number two, because my palm made contact with his bare chest. That one touch went straight to my core. My damn clit throbbed, joining the vajayjay uprising in trying to take over my life.

"No one is peeing on anyone."

elik

MY MATE WAS BEAUTIFUL. Her long brown hair had been pulled back into some kind of layered knot that clearly revealed strands of red hiding among them. Her eyes were green and gold. I wanted to drown in them.

The scent of her arousal made it nearly impossible to remain in control. The beast could smell her, too. And he'd been waiting for so long. So fucking long.

She was younger than I had imagined my mate would be, but the beast had chosen and I could not fault his instincts. *Stefani.*

Mate. Mine. The beast sounded smug, which was much better than the angry killer I'd been dealing with less than an hour ago.

Ours. I reminded him as I watched her search inside her bag, remove a bottle of some sort and repeatedly press and squeeze the thing.

The male who accompanied her was no threat. I could crush him without effort.

Crush. Yes. My beast was all over that one, his protective instincts so strong the male was nearly dead before he'd taken his next breath.

He is important to our mate. She will be angry with us if we hurt him.

The beast was not pleased, but he stopped imagining the young male torn in half, pieces floating in the water next to the pier.

Violent fucker.

Mine.

Yes, I know. Patience. We don't want to scare her.

Fuck, not scare. Pleasure. I'd never heard my beast like this. We fought in the war. We hunted. We killed. We had, in the past, fucked willing females when we found one pleasing enough. Never had I heard my beast...purr.

The annoying sting on my legs was irrelevant. I did not know why my mate was fussing so, but I enjoyed being cared for by my female, so I did not inform her that the little sea creatures' attacks barely registered.

Until the male mentioned urinating on me.

Told you. Kill him. The beast growled at him and took a step forward with the intention of ripping the male to pieces.

One touch from our female and we both stopped cold.

"No one is peeing on anyone." My mate's tone was meant to be stern. I found her to be...enchanting.

"I will allow you to do anything you wish, my lady." I bent my arm to place my hand on top of hers where her light touch pressed to my chest. My words were no lie. She was mine to serve, to protect, to pleasure. Anything she needed, I would provide. All she need do was ask.

"Oh, god." Stefani tugged to escape my hold on her hand. I did not let her go. I could not. "No. No, thank you."

"Told you. I want one." The female, Carmen, grinned at me and walked past both Stefani and me. "I'm going home. Have fun, you two!"

The male jogged after her. "Hey! Wait up! You're my ride."

"Guys!" Stefani shouted, but the two humans wisely ignored her and continued their journey. She was mine now. I would not tolerate interference.

My mate sighed and looked up at me. "You're a mess. You know that, right?"

Chaos consumed me as my entire existence shifted to her. Unable to resist another moment, I lifted my free hand to stroke the softness of her cheek with gentle fingertips. "You are beautiful, mate." That smallest of touches made my head spin. I was literally...dizzy.

Mind swirling, I adjusted my stance so I would not fall over and focused on my mate's voice.

"I don't want a mate. Nothing against you, Velik. I'm sure you're wonderful. I just...what a disaster." Her words made my stomach lurch in a way I had never experienced before. Was this what the others meant when they said a mate made one weak? Vulnerable? I had thought they played a word game, not that I would literally watch the world spin, feel my stomach heave.

She wrapped her small hand around mine and drew my fingers away from her face. "Come on. I'll take you back to the processing center. You live there, right?"

"I have quarters there." *Our quarters.* I did not say the second part aloud.

She pulled again and I reluctantly released the hand she had pressed to my chest. Once free, she stepped back and looked me up and down. "I'm not sure you will fit in my car."

"I will fit." I would fold my frame into her human contraption, or I would carry her home. Either was fine with me. I was a warlord. I would care for and claim my mate in whatever manner was required. She would never be out of my sight again.

Mine.

Got it, beast. Ours. And he was very pleased with the thought of staying within sight of our mate forever. Within reach would be better...

"Okay. If you say so. Come on. I have tweezers in my car."

Her command was unnecessary. I was not familiar with these *tweezers,* but I would follow her anywhere until the day I died. Obviously, she did not yet understand what it meant to be mine.

The distance to her vehicle was short. Soon we walked across hot black tar that had hardened to cover the ground. I assumed this was so the human cars would not sink too deeply into the sand. As with the humans' roads, the method was inefficient but seemed to work for them.

Row upon row of cars waited for their owners to return. I wondered which one belonged to my female.

She walked to the very end of a row, stopped, looked me up and down and shook her head. "One problem at a time."

After digging around in the large bag hanging from her shoulder, she pulled a small black item free and pointed it at the tiny car until it beeped. The rear window section of the vehicle rose slowly, on some kind of automated system. Stefani tossed her bag into the back of the vehicle, leaned in, and pulled a second, completely different style of bag toward her.

Her long legs were perfectly toned and curved. Her thighs looked soft to touch. The small skirt she wore rose as she leaned forward, and I saw...

My cock pulsed with pain. Her bare ass with nothing but a thin, pink slip of fabric separating the round lobes. Soft. Smooth. I wanted to touch. Grab. Pull her ass cheeks apart, spread her pussy lips wide, make room for my cock to pump in and out of her.

I was going to die, right here. My cock was going to explode. I would bleed to death, which would be acceptable, as long as I could fuck her as I bled out.

She smiled at me over her shoulder and the throbbing pain migrated from my cock to my chest—and squeezed.

"Navy SEALS have their Go-Bags. Well, so do single ladies." She pulled a backpack toward her and yanked items loose, dropping them next to the pack as she went. "Shoes. Hah. Definitely don't need those. Little black dress. Hair—ah! Found it."

What she had in her hand was a sparkling green pouch. She unzipped the closure and pulled a small metal item free before turning to me.

"Emergency make-up bag to the rescue. I prefer waxing my eyebrows or threading, but backup tweezers are a must have." She lifted the slender item and squeezed in the center. The two tips met at the end. "I'm sure you're a great guy, but those tentacles are not coming in my car."

Without explanation, she crouched down in front of me. From a nearby park, a human male whistled a crude sound. I let my beast roar back and the young male turned and ran.

No one insulted my mate, nor attempted to torment or embarrass her.

"Ignore him. Just your standard asshole."

"My mate will not suffer assholes, standard or otherwise."

"God, you're as bad as Max." Stefani pressed the end of her tweezers to my leg and lifted a small strand of what had once been attached to the sea creature from my leg. The stinging sensation did not lessen, but I cared not. The pain was a mere pittance. Actually, a boon, as my mate now tended to me.

I must walk into the ocean and find these creatures more often.

Barely daring to move as my mate pulled what she referred to as *tentacles* from my flesh, I ground my teeth and held back a groan as she forgot herself and placed her bare palm against my leg.

My head spun yet again, and I grabbed on to the edge of her car for balance.

If her touch had this effect, fucking her might kill me.

Fuck her now. Mine.

Swallowing a groan as she moved her hand slightly and targeted yet another tentacle, I told my beast to shut up. She was human. I could not simply throw her down on the ground, lift that tiny pink skirt and...

Yes! Claim!

I staggered as the beast fought me for control. I had gone too far, pushed myself too close to the edge. I was not sure I could control him.

Stefani paused what she was doing and looked up at me. Her hand remained pressed to my thigh. "Are you alright?"

"No." I needed her to touch me everywhere. My cock was especially eager, hard and reaching for her in a very obvious manner from beneath my shorts.

She dipped her chin at my response and promptly gasped at the proximity of her mouth to the eager length. I envisioned her kneeling before me, as she did now, her lips wrapped around my hard cock as she held my balls with one hand and clenched my thigh with the other, anchored to me.

Her fingertips were painted a bright yellow and I envisioned those fingertips digging into my shoulders as I claimed her. As if she could read my mind, her cheeks darkened in hue to a colorful pink.

Gods she was beautiful.

"Umm, you can't look at me like that."

"How am I looking at you? You are beautiful. I desire you. I am proud to be your mate."

"Shhh. Just...turn around."

I followed her command because if I had not, the beast would have lifted her from the ground and shoved her pussy on top of us, slid her small, wet—oh yes, she was wet and ready, for I could still smell her heat—pussy up and down the throbbing length until I exploded inside her, filled her with seed.

A shudder raced over my flesh, through my core. The unease in my gut shifted angrily within, making me feel sick with need, a brutal reminder of how close I was to losing complete control.

No. No. Fuck no. I would not force my female. I would *not*. I'd fucking survived mating fever for this long. I could hold on for a few more hours, or days—gods forbid—if that was what my mate needed to feel safe and protected.

With a growl rumbling through me, I presented her with the backs of my legs and thighs. I felt the press of her small metal device and waited for her to be satisfied.

"Oh, shit."

"What is it?" I turned at once, ready to kill to protect her.

"There are a couple hanging out of your shorts."

"That is not a problem, mate." More than willing to present my body for her inspection—and, I hoped, approval —I yanked the material from my hips, tearing the fragile seams in seconds. Not wanting to risk any of the offending tentacles making contact with her vehicle—and upsetting her—I threw the offending shorts a significant distance away.

"Oh, god! What are you—" She jumped upright and dove for the large bag she had thrown into her car earlier. Tugging quickly, she pulled a long piece of fabric free. This was a beach towel. I was familiar with a number of human items. Stefani's towel had a large cartoon depiction of the sun with a smiling face in its center. Cheerful. Bright. Like her.

She held it out to me with one hand covering her eyes. "Here."

Confused, I gently removed the towel from her hand. I was not wet.

"Is it safe?"

Her question confused me.

"Of course." I would not tolerate any threat to her and was acutely aware of our surroundings. Several humans, seated on cracking wooden benches farther down the walking path, pointed in our direction. They appeared to be laughing at us, but they were small and weak, and had no weapons.

Stefani lowered her hand from her face, her cheeks now more red than pink. Interesting. The shade had spread to her neck as well. I laid her sunshine towel over my bent elbow and reached for her.

"Are you unwell?"

"I'm fine. God. You're supposed to cover up with that."

"Cover up? What am I to cover?"

She squeaked. "Yourself."

I glanced at the small towel in disbelief. "This is not large enough to cover me, my lady. Although I will attempt to do as you wish." I held the towel by the corners to judge its length. No, it would not cover even half of my torso. Still, my mate seemed to think it important, and I wanted to please her.

I swung the towel around behind me to cover the back of my shoulders, my hips, ass and the tops of my thighs. That was the best I could do.

"Is this better, mate?"

"No. It's not a cape." She turned to the side as she reached for the towel. Her hand brushed my hard cock before gently slapping against my abdomen. My hard length jumped in reaction. My beast groaned.

Stefani sprang back as if burned. "Oh, god. I'm sorry. I just—I—never mind." The reddish tone of her skin had not abated. Perhaps my beautiful female was suffering the same frustration and desire as I.

"I can give you pleasure now, mate." I turned my back to any who might be watching—still covered by the cape, as she'd called it—and took a step toward her. She backed up until her thighs came into contact with her car.

"What? No, that's crazy." She looked around as if expecting an attack.

"No one will harm you. I give you my word, female. Anyone who might interfere with your pleasure will die."

"You can't just go around killing people, Velik."

"I will eliminate any threat to you." Bending down, I leaned forward until our faces nearly touched.

"You're supposed to wrap that around your waist." Stefani lifted her gaze to the towel I held in place over my shoulder.

Ah. That made much more sense. I stood to my full height—making sure to display my hard cock to my female —and wrapped the towel around my hips.

I looked down to judge her reaction. I wanted to entice and seduce her. I needed her to desire me, not fear me.

Her breathing was shallow and too fast. She was rubbing her hands up and down her thighs as if irritated or nervous. And her skin? Bright red.

Was she feverish? Too hot?

"Are you unwell? You must answer truthfully, or I will not be able to properly care for you."

"I'm fine." She licked her lips and I watched without blinking, hypnotized by the small action. My pulse pounded in my ears. I fought the urge to lift her from the ground, tear her clothing from her body, thrust into her pussy. Claim her here. Now. Right fucking now.

This female was going to own me. "I want to taste your pussy, mate. I need to taste you."

"We're in a parking lot. In broad daylight."

"Mine." The beast's low rumble was back as he fought me for control. If he took over now, I wouldn't be able to stop him. He would not surrender to me until he'd fucked her. Claimed her.

Or we were dead. There would be no other option for us should she refuse to accept our claim. Our body. We needed our mate to find us worthy and make us whole.

"This is insane."

No being had ever spoken truer words.

Her hands moved at a more languid pace, up and down her thighs. Knees to hips. Back and forth. The scent of her wet pussy called to me, and the beast inhaled deeply, savoring the scent, wanting to taste her.

Not want. Need.

I needed to touch her, too.

"I need—" Fuck. How was I going to explain the primitive needs of my beast to this perfect female? My beast growled when I did not finish my statement. I couldn't speak our truth. *Shut the fuck up beast. Do you want to scare her?*

"What? I know there are a couple more tentacles under that towel. I can get them off now."

"No. I need—I—*fuck*..." I couldn't speak my desire. Didn't dare. If she refused me, the beast would rage, and I would not be able to stop him. I was too close to the edge. Instead, I dropped down and knelt before her. Small pieces of gravel pierced the skin of my knees where they rested on the ground. I welcomed the pain. I needed it to maintain control.

"What are you doing?" She scooted back until her bottom rested on the odd carpeting inside the back of her car. Her knees hung over the edge, her tiny feet nowhere near touching the ground.

With a sound I feared would remind her of a wounded animal, I bent over and placed my head in her lap, the top of my scalp pressed to her stomach, my face atop her thighs, my shoulders leaning on her knees. I held most of my weight away from her slight frame, but I needed this. Contact. Connection.

My beast couldn't be alone anymore.

"I'm sorry." I spoke into the crease between her thighs even as I breathed in the exotic scent of her pussy. I was so close to her wet heat. So close. In and out of my lungs. My mate's wet cream. My home. So close.

I knew I should get up, move away. No doubt I was being too forward for this human female. If she were an Atlan female, I would have tossed her over my shoulder, carried her to a private area, transformed into my beast and fucked her mindless by now. She would be begging for more. The liquid fire of her pussy juices would be on my lips and tongue, down my throat, and coating my cock.

But Stefani was small and human. Fragile. I had to proceed with utmost care, so I did not terrorize her into rejecting me. And yet...

I pressed my lips to the bare skin of her inner thigh. Barely made contact. Gently brushed the taste of her skin onto my lips.

My entire body shuddered, and I lifted my arms into the car so I could slide my hands around behind her and hold her tight. She was so small. One of my hands nearly covered her entire back. Desperate for more contact, I slipped my hand under the hem of her plain white shirt. Her back was soft as silk and bare to my touch except for a thin bit of string tied into a knot in the center. Touching her was addictive. Palm flat, my touch roamed from the base of her neck to the waist of her short, pink skirt.

The other hand I wrapped around her hip, my fingers covering as much of her ass as I could while she sat there. I squeezed the soft, round flesh. Ached to bury my rock hard cock deep. Touching her hurt me, my longing a physical pain.

I rubbed my cheek against the inside of one thigh as I kissed the other. She lifted her hands to my head and buried her fingers in my hair.

"I can't believe you guys are for real."

"I am real, mate. And you are mine."

Her sigh did not please my beast. "We'll talk about that later, after I get you home and you get all those jellyfish stings taken care of."

"No. Now." My beast rose from the depths of my soul, terrified that our female thought to deny us. Escape us.

Find me—us—unworthy.

Pleasure now.

Oh fuck, no. I argued with him. The beast was beyond caring what I thought.

He took control, slid my hand gently from her hip and moved it around to cup her breast.

She gasped, but the nipple was pebbled and hard. Her pussy grew wetter, the smell an instant aphrodisiac that did nothing to discourage him.

"We're in a parking lot." Stefani whispered the words, as if speaking them softly would make them untrue.

"Yes." The beast didn't give a fuck where we were, as long as we were with her. His deep rumble made her hands fist in my hair. Or perhaps it was the soft tug on her nipple. "Taste. Now." The beast nudged her thighs with his nose, wanting her to open to us. Let us in.

"Velik."

Her legs relaxed just enough to encourage him. He pressed closer and buried his face close to her feminine heat. Her lusty scent stole every protest from me, mind and body.

Taste her. I was the one making silent demands now, locked away in my mind. The beast was in control. Gods help us all, she was his now. I wouldn't be able to stop him.

He was gone. Owned. Addicted. There would never be another female for him. For us. Taste her?

He chuckled as if I was an idiot.

4

 tefani

I was in serious trouble here. Serious. Trouble.

Shit. I was so turned on I was behaving badly. I had the sexiest man alive all over me in the parking lot. In broad daylight. His hand on my breast made me want to lean in closer. His hot breath coated my clit in a steady rhythm that made it impossible to think.

That was a lie.

I was thinking all right. All kinds of thoughts. Just that none of them involved sitting up, pushing him away and driving him safely back to Miami.

No. More like his tongue buried deep inside me, pushing me to an orgasm followed by his huge cock stretching me wide. I would come in two seconds flat. I was that close already.

Damn it. This was not part of my plan. I wasn't supposed to love any—

His tongue flicked out and dove between my legs, stroking my clit through the thin material of my suit like he had an advanced clitoris targeting radar system. Maybe he did, because he did it again. And again.

Shit.

I wasn't a horny teenager. I could control myself.

Determined to save myself from public humiliation—and save him from being arrested and thrown in federal prison for walking around planet Earth without the proper, what — Permit? I tugged on his hair. Hard.

He moved quickly, too fast for me to realize I'd made a fatal error.

He knelt before me, his hand still on my breast. His face now even with mine. "Velik. We can't—"

With a grin I had no hope of denying, he leaned forward and took my lips. Claimed them. His tongue moved into my mouth and tasted me, moving so I could think of nothing else but his cock following along with a matching rhythm downtown.

First he stomps around naked—and gorgeous. Now he kisses like this?

Velik's kiss was like lightning, jolting me awake and pushing away any thoughts rambling around in my head. His lips took everything, devoured me. Marked me. I instantly lost a battle against something I could not control.

Want. Need. The great big, aching hole in my heart that never seemed to go away. Always hurting and bleeding and waiting for the next person I loved to disappear.

Velik's strong hand gripped my neck, pulling me closer even though I should have backed away. His huge body surrounded me with his power, taunted me with its promise of safety. Loyalty. A promise of forever that my analytical heart knew no one would ever be able to keep.

He would break me, make me want and dream and truly believe he was mine. For a moment, I let myself imagine it. I gave in. I kissed him back.

I wrapped both arms around his head and pulled him down to me. I never could have moved him on my own, but he came willingly, pressed closer and wrapped an arm around my waist. He pulled me against him until our bodies melted into one another and his heat flooded my system like a drug.

His taste made me dizzy, like I was stumbling through darkness, unable to find a way out. I forgot who I was. Who he was. The list of reasons I'd memorized of why a relationship like this would never, ever work for me.

Our tongues explored and tangled. My back landed on the carpeting in the back of my car but I didn't care. Far off, in the distance, I heard whistling and shouting. I ignored everything but him. I didn't have a choice. He was everywhere, surrounding me, over me, holding me, making me want to forget.

Somehow, he'd followed me into the back of my car. He was on top of me, had shifted our bodies so that I was inside while his legs remained out.

The towel he'd wrapped around his hips brushed my inner thighs like sandpaper when I wanted skin. His skin.

He'd gone beast. I felt his shoulders grow, heard the low, rumbling growl as he licked between my thighs to stroke my clit.

Velik was out of his mind with need. For me. Only me. In the entire universe I was the only woman he would ever want like this.

The knowledge slammed into me like a drug. I wrapped my legs around his hips. Power made my blood heat. He was mine. I'd been lying to myself purely out of self-preservation. I didn't dare hope for a warlord of my own. Did. Not. Dare.

I couldn't allow myself to think it because, if it hadn't happened? I would have had a broken heart.

But now he was here. He was mine. My heart broke anyway. Crushed with hope. That this was real. That I could keep him.

I was going to fucking keep him.

Reaching between us, I tugged at the towel around his hips until it opened in the front and took the head of his cock into my hand.

The beast, *my* beast went stiff with shock, but I didn't dare give him time to change his mind. Using my legs, which I wrapped around his hips to keep the rest of the towel in place covering his ass, I lifted my hips until I could pull the g-string of my pink bikini to the side with the same hand that held his cock and guided him to my wet heat. I pressed the head of his cock to my entrance but could not get him all the way inside. I wanted him stretching me open. Invading my body. Sliding into my tight pussy and making me burn to adjust, to take all of him.

"Claim me, Velik. Do it." I needed this to be real. Final. If I was going to let my heart splinter with the pain of hope, of believing his obsession would last forever, he was going to have to make me forget all my doubts. He had to fill me up. Thrust deep. I had to be part of him, or I was going to shatter into a million little pieces of broken glass. It was too late now. He'd said the word. That freaking word.

"Mine." I thought the beast would push forward into my pussy as he spoke. Instead, he tugged at the buttons on my shirt until they popped open to reveal my bikini clad breasts. His hand spread wide over my chest, settling just under my jaw. Skin to skin. Holding me in place. A primitive part of me took over and I arched my neck, thrust my breasts toward him.

"Velik, please." Please shove your cock deep. Please lay your weight on top of me so I can barely move. Please fuck me hard and fast and make my body explode like a firework.

I knew beasts generally claimed their mates in a standing position. It was instinctive. They were always alert, ready to kill to protect their female. I had learned a lot about them, enough to know Velik's beast might not have sex with me like this. Here. Now. In the back of my goddamn car like a couple of high school idiots.

"I need you inside me." I whispered the confession with a voice I'd never heard before. Raw, unfiltered me. No fear. No games. Absolute honesty.

As if I'd broken something inside him, his entire body shifted. I cried out as his cock filled me in one hard thrust. He slipped a hand under my hips and lifted my ass just enough, tilted my body so he could go deeper. Harder. Fuck me faster without having to fight to move in the small confines of my car.

Velik's claiming was like riding lightning. Every sense was filled with him. He was all I could see. Feel. Hear. Smell. He surrounded me and was buried deep inside me. The beast fucked me like an animal, almost out of control. I wasn't sure if he would ever stop, his wildness pushing me over the edge until my keening cries echoed inside the car like a blasting stereo. I didn't want his beast to fuck me in the car, I *needed* it, and he gave me what I needed even if it meant going against his instinct. My heart was in my throat as I cried out.

I didn't care who saw us, who heard me. Did. Not. Care. My inner walls were shooting off like a supernova, every spasm clamping down on his cock while his bulk held the small muscles wide, stretched open, burning up as his invasion pushed my orgasm higher. Next level. Nothing existed but him.

It seemed to go on forever. Time had no meaning as he pumped his seed into me and his soft groans filled the car.

When it was over, he lay pressed on top of me, breathing heavily. His skin was hot. Blazing hot. I would have to ask Adrian if all Atlans got this way during sex, or if it was just *my* Atlan.

My Atlan. I liked the sound of that.

I lay unmoving for a few minutes, fingers shifting through the soft strands of his hair. I liked this feeling, could get addicted; his body still inside me, ripples of aftershocks pulsing through my core. His heat kept me warm like a protective blanket. A very satisfied man—alien—practically passed out with pleasure on top of me.

"Velik?"

"Hmmm." His response was more rumble than anything.

"Your ass is hanging out the back of my car. We should probably get out of here and get your jellyfish stings looked at." The aliens could use their magical healing wand on him and then we could do this again. And again.

I remembered now. Adrian had recommended keeping a Re-Gen wand handy for taking care of soreness after...well. She had an Atlan mate, too.

Reaching up, over my head, I stroked his cheek. His lips were full and kissable. Everything about him was perfect. His eyes were closed and he looked like a little boy. Well, a very large boy.

Scratch that. There was nothing boyish left in the beast's face. He just looked...at peace. I did that for him. Me. It seemed impossible. "Hey there, big guy. Did I wear you out already?"

Silence. Not even a flicker of his eyelids. Nothing.

With every ounce of strength I possessed, I shoved him until he rolled onto his side next to me and I could wiggle out from beneath him. His back hit the wheel well with a thud. Dead weight. Legs hanging out the back of the car.

Oh, god. What was wrong with him? Why wasn't he moving?

"Velik? Velik!"

5

"COME ON, COME ON, COME ON!" I held down the horn as I raced past another red light. I'd never broken so many traffic laws in my life. I'd barely managed to get Velik's legs into the car. God, he was heavy. But I did it. I had no idea what was wrong with him, but I couldn't exactly take him to a human hospital.

Here's a three hundred pound alien, doc. Fix him up.

No. His only chance was the processing center. They had ReGen tech there and doctors who knew how to treat a Warlord without killing him. And it wasn't that far now.

Velik's silence pushed me close to a pure panic. I turned on the radio so I would be able to finish the drive. Without the noise I would have spent every second of the drive listening to see if I could hear him breathing.

Please be breathing.

Did Atlans have heart attacks? Or strokes? Maybe an

aneurysm? Did they just topple over like humans did? Or
was it the damn jellyfish stings? That many on a human
definitely would have earned a hospital visit. But he'd
seemed fine. *More* than fine.

Hot. Sexy. Growly and possessive in the most delicious
way. I'd never allowed myself to really believe I'd have a
mate like my sister did. The possibility of it never
happening was too painful. So, I just didn't hope.

Until there he was, saying *'mine',* and blowing my mind,
taking me in public. What's more? I didn't care who saw us.
Which had been oddly...liberating. And sexy.

Was I turning into a freak now who got off on having sex
in public?

What if I was? Did I care?

No. I didn't. I only cared about him. He was mine now,
my mate. My forever. He'd said the word and he'd claimed
me. I knew how the Atlan beast worked. One woman and
that was it. One and done. He. Was. Mine.

The tires on my car squealed around the turn as I
hauled ass into the Interstellar Brides Center parking lot.
There was a guard, of course. I slammed on the brakes, fish-
tailed toward him and didn't feel one bit sorry when he had
to take a step back to avoid being hit by the car's bumper. I
rolled down my window to the smell of burning tires on
asphalt. "I have Velik. He's in a coma or something. He
needs a doctor."

The guard *looked* human, more human than the
warlords did, but there was something about him that made
my spidey-senses tingle. We'd found out, when Adrian
tracked down Kovo before she even saw him, that we had a
bit of Everian Hunter blood in our family line somewhere.
As soon as I thought it, I knew. Yep. This guy was from
Everis.

He sniffed the air—smelling for Velik?—before nodding. "Follow me."

The guard took off at a dead run and, yes. Totally from Everis. He ran as fast as my car could maneuver through the parking lot to follow him. Somehow, I knew that if he needed to, he could move even faster.

He led me to a set of large sliding doors along the back of one of the sprawling complex's buildings. I parked and hit the button to lift the hatch. A group of large aliens ran outside before I even got out of the car.

Watching them lift Velik like he weighed no more than a child was...disconcerting. They were all big. Strong. A couple Prillon warriors, the Everian who had led me inside, and a beast that looked like he wanted to kill something.

He probably did.

The Everian Hunter returned to me as the others disappeared inside with Velik. I moved forward to follow but the guard blocked my path. "Apologies, my lady, but we will need some information before you may enter."

I wanted to slap him and stomp past him, but I wouldn't get even one step past this guy. "Fine. But talk fast. I need to get in there." To Velik. My mate. I needed to be with him when the doctor or their scanner or whatever they had figured out what was *wrong* with him.

"Who are you?"

"Stefani Davis."

"Human."

"Yes."

"You live in Miami?"

"Yes."

"How was Velik injured?"

"I don't know. He just passed out."

"How did you know to bring him here?"

Really? I stopped watching the doors my mate had disappeared behind and stared into the intense eyes of the very polite—asshole—who was in my way. I could barely focus over my hand-twisting anxiety. He'd just outrun my car and wasn't even breathing hard. Jerk.

"Look, Hunter man. My name is Stefani Davis. My mother is Vivian Davis, mate of Warlord Maxus. My sister is Adrian Davis, mate to Warlord Kovo. I have been to Atlan, more than once, and I know a beast when I see one. He seemed perfectly fine—" More than fine, actually, but I didn't want to discuss my sex life with this alien. "He was fine. And then, he just stopped moving. Stopped talking. I have no idea what happened to him. I need to get in there so I can find out."

"How did someone of your...petite stature get the warlord into your car?"

I was going to slap him. "With difficulty. Now get out of my way."

"Elite Hunter Rowan, thank you. I will take it from here." A woman's voice carried across the open area and I turned to see Warden Egara walking toward us. Thank god. Someone reasonable. "Stefani, what a surprise. I hadn't expected to see you again so soon."

Warden Egara walked to stand between me and *Elite Hunter Rowan.*

Called it.

He bowed slightly to Warden Egara and then to me. "Ladies, it has been an honor." Then he was...gone. Like, vampire movie, superhero gone. Poofed into thin air. I gasped.

The warden laughed. "They are fast, aren't they?"

"Holy shit."

My response made her laugh harder. She wrapped her

hand around my arm and gently led me toward the entry doors. "Now, tell me what has happened. Are you well?" She looked me over from head to toe and I realized I was still in beach wear. Hot pink bikini with tiny skirt covering a barely-there G-string bottom. The white cotton button-up I'd worn over it had lost most of the buttons when Velik—yeah. Anyway, it didn't button anymore. And I'd spent the entire afternoon with my hair blowing in the wind on the bow of a sailboat...or gone wild in the back of my car like a horny teenager.

I was a mess. No wonder Rowan had looked at me like I was suspect.

"What happened to Velik?"

"I don't know. I ran into him at the pier. He was covered in jellyfish stings and he was really far away from where he was supposed to be. I didn't want him to get in trouble."

"Thank you for bringing him back discreetly. He has been...troubled lately."

"He was running on the beach. Guess he went into the water at some point. There were signs all over the beach today about the jellies, but knowing Max and Kovo, Velik wouldn't have paid attention to them anyway."

She chuckled. "No, he would not."

"Anyway, we walked to my car. I used some tweezers to pull the rest of the tentacles off him."

"And that's why he was naked?"

Where was a hole and how fast could I sink into it? "Some of them were, umm, under his clothes. When I mentioned seeing one sticking out, he just stripped naked right there in the parking lot."

"Of course."

"He was fine. Talking and walking and...stuff. And then he just stopped. Like he passed out between one second and the next." The memory of shaking him, trying to wake him up, made me shiver. "I had to make a sling with the beach towel to get him the rest of the way into my car. I got him in and drove here as fast as I could."

As we'd talked, the warden had led me inside to some sort of viewing room. A large window separated us from what was going on in the next room as a doctor in green scanned and poked and prodded Velik, issuing instructions to two others in with him to move his unconscious body here or there. "Why isn't he in a ReGen pod yet?""

"I don't know." Warden Egara walked up next to me. We stood silent, shoulder to shoulder, and watched the medical team work on him. The doctor seemed particularly interested in the streaks caused by the jellyfish tentacles. And no wonder, they covered almost half of Velik's legs.

It felt like an eternity, but my trusty watch told me it had been no more than ten minutes since they'd pulled Velik out of the back of my car.

Self-conscious now that things weren't in all out panic mode, I pulled my white shirt around me to cover up the best I could.

A few minutes later I held my breath as they lifted Velik into a ReGen pod and closed the lid. The doctor looked up at us then, his gaze locking with Warden Egara's before he looked at me. When she nodded he walked out of the suite.

Less than a minute later he was standing in front of me.

"You brought him in?"

"Yes."

"The red lesions beneath the skin on his legs, do you know what caused them?"

"They aren't under his skin. They're jellyfish stings."

"How is one attacked by these creatures?"

I shrugged. "By swimming in the ocean. They're everywhere. There was a notice on the beach today, warning people not to get in the water."

"Hmmph. Are these creatures venomous?"

"I—yes—I guess. Not like a rattlesnake or anything. Most of the time we just put some spray on them and take a shower. Unless you get stung by a lot of them."

The doctor pulled a computer tablet of some kind from his pocket. Within seconds I saw images of jellyfish moving across the small screen. "Fuck. There are more than two thousand sub-species?"

"I don't know. I'm not a marine biologist."

He looked at me like I was a bug under his shoe, like Velik's condition—and the fact that the Earth had so many different kinds of jellyfish—was completely my fault. "I need a sample of the species that attacked him."

"They don't attack. They just sting you if you get in their way."

"Either way, the poison is not one we have encountered before. It is having previously unseen effects on Velik's nervous system."

"What does that mean?" I asked.

"He's dying. I need a raw sample of the creature's venom. If I don't get a raw sample, I can't create an antidote."

I froze like marble. Die? He was dying?

"How long does he have, doctor?" Warden Egara asked.

"The ReGen pod is repairing the damage, but the venom is not breaking down in his system. It's...mutating into something else. The poison will continue to kill cells in his body at nearly the same rate our ReGen pod can heal them."

"Do you need the entire jellyfish? Or just a tentacle with the poison?" I had a pretty good idea where I could get a tentacle or two.

"I need the poison in its original form. The creature is of no concern."

"Will the pod thing keep him alive while I go get one?"

"Yes, barring another unexpected reaction."

I didn't want to know the mechanics of Velik's *unexpected* reaction. A detailed explanation would just freak me out. The pod was going to keep Velik alive and I was going to go get this doctor a freaking jellyfish tentacle if I had to go out into the ocean and bring back one of the damn things attached to my skin. "I'll be right back."

The doctor nodded. I turned and took one more look at Velik under the closed pod's translucent covering. An Atlan warlord. The most feared fighter in the Coalition Fleet. A beast. And he was dying because his body had a nasty reaction to a stupid little creature, smaller than my fist, that floated around in the ocean.

God. He looked so peaceful in the healing pod. A real Snow White in the forest moment. Except this time the handsome prince had taken a bite of the poisoned apple and I was going to kiss him better no matter how many stupid jellyfish I had to catch.

I was not going to lose him like I'd lost everyone else. I couldn't do it. I really, really didn't think I could mentally survive losing my happily-ever-after before I even had a chance to live it.

elik, Forty-Eight Hours Later

I KNEW the inside of a ReGen pod when I saw one. This one was new, barely a scratch on the cover. Not that a disoriented warlord had ever pounded a few of them with his fists. Only the Prillon warriors did that.

Eyes closed, I took stock. I felt great. Calm. At peace. My beast seemed to be...subdued and content. A shock, as I'd been fighting him night and day for months. Now?

Quiet.

Thank the gods.

The lid to the enclosure slid open and Doctor Mersan stood over me. "What are you doing here?" He was an Intelligence Core specialist, more likely to be found fucking around inside someone's head—literally—than babysitting a standard ReGen pod. He'd saved my life many times, but he wasn't supposed to be here, on Earth.

"Helion sent me. Wanted to make sure you survived."

"Survived what?" I couldn't remember a fucking thing. Nothing. I'd been running on the beach, as I'd done dozens of times before. Then...waking up here.

"Apparently, warlord, your kind has a deadly reaction to one of this planet's small sea creatures. It's called a jellyfish." He turned and raised one hand to indicate a clear jar where a nearly translucent blob floated in a clear fluid.

"What?" I stared at the creature. It was smaller than my hand. No exoskeleton. No bones. "*That thing* almost killed me?"

"Indeed." The Prillon doctor stood next to my pod, his face his usual emotionless mask. "Can you sit?"

I felt fine. "Of course." I sat up and swung my legs over the edge. I was naked, which was standard procedure. I was not modest. Even if I was, this Prillon had seen me this way dozens, if not hundreds, of times.

Alarm spiked through me when the room spun. "Fuck!" I grabbed the edge of the ReGen pod and held myself upright. Barely. Without my hold on the pod I would have ended up flat on the floor. "What the fuck?"

"As I suspected. Just sit there for a couple minutes while I do some tests." Doctor Mersan moved efficiently, holding one small device after another near my head.

"What is wrong with me?"

"It appears the venom in the jellyfish destroyed a substantial number of neurons in your brain. The peripheral nerves appear to be less effected."

"What the fuck does that mean?"

"It means, warlord, that although we managed to stop the poison from killing you, certain areas of your brain had to be rebuilt by the ReGen pod. A few of your motor neurons were damaged and are still healing."

I opened my mouth to bark another question, but

Mersan lifted his hand to stop me. "You're going to be fine. It will just take a few more hours in ReGen to heal the rest of the way."

Thank the gods. This was a fucking nightmare. To survive years in the war to be taken down by a blob of jelly? Fucking humiliating.

"All of your long term memory is intact. Your battle training and history should all be in place." He glared at me. "Rogue 5?"

Ah. A test.

"Latiri 4?"

"Deep cave Hive base. Tore it to pieces."

Mersan nodded. "Battleship Zeus?"

"Female Hive hybrid battleship. First of her kind."

"Excellent. As I suspected, it is only your recent, short-term memory that has been affected." He was actually grinning now. "Once you can stand up without falling over—"

I growled a warning out of habit. My beast did not particularly like this Prillon. With good reason. He'd done a lot of...medical procedures on us when we were still active in the I.C..

"No offense intended, Warlord Velik. To you or your beast."

I settled back, confused. I was irritated with the doctor, but where was my beast? Why wasn't I arguing with him about whether or not to rip this arrogant Prillon's head off his shoulders?

I searched within for the beast as the doctor rambled on. I would receive a formal briefing later, I had no doubt. And the doctor's voice tended to be...annoying.

There he was. Almost...asleep? *What are you doing?*

My beast stared at me like I was an idiot.

At least that felt normal.

Do you need me to kill something for you? I did not sense danger.

No.

Then fuck off.

What the fuck was going on here? I studied my beast for a few moments. He appeared to be perfectly fine, if in a bad mood. Which was completely normal.

"Warlord, did you hear me? You will be transporting to I.C. Core command within the hour. You will finish your healing there and meet up with your team." Doctor Mersan pressed an injector of some kind against my neck. The medication burned, but the sensation only lasted a few seconds, replaced with a surge of energy I sorely needed. My head cleared. The dizziness abated.

I turned my head to each side, stretching tendons and loosening stiff muscles as much as I could.

Oh yes. This routine I knew well. Helion needed me to do something for him. No doubt it would involve rending, tearing, hunting and killing our enemies. "Excellent. I am ready now."

I was tired of this planet. These people. Being locked inside the grounds of the processing center because the humans were too afraid of us to allow us to walk among them.

The door to the medical bay slid open and Warden Egara walked in. I did not cover up, but she did not look me over.

Pity. She was an attractive female.

My beast grunted disagreement. As usual. Not interested.

"He is not to leave before we address the issue of the young woman in my office, Doctor. I believe I made that clear."

"Perfectly." The doctor turned away from the warden so only I could see his face. He looked...annoyed. "Nothing will come of it. She is lying."

"I do not believe that for one minute." Warden Egara placed her hands on her hips. Her scowl would have scared her Prillon mates, if she still had them. The tragedy of their deaths was often whispered about in the I.C..

"Warlord Velik, I have a young woman here who claims she is your mate."

"I have no mate." My beast barely stirred. He agreed.

"And your beast? What does he say? I want to talk to him."

Pushy female. The beast was nearly as annoyed as I, but he responded, rising to the surface and partially transforming my face. "Warden."

"Beast. Do you confirm this? Do you not have a mate?"

"No. No mate." He shrank back inside me and the warden watched him go, her gray eyes suddenly cloudy with emotion. Females did not make sense. This did not concern her. She was not my mate. Why was she so upset? She looked at the doctor.

"And he is one hundred percent healed? His beast is fully functional? His body healed?"

"Yes. He needs a few more hours in the ReGen pod to heal the remainder of his peripheral nerve damage, but that is all. He is battle ready."

"Shit."

Why was she cursing me?

"As the warden in charge of this brides' testing facility, I require further proof." She glared at Doctor Mersan, then turned those gray eyes back to me. "You will put some clothing on, Warlord. Then you will report to my office. Do you understand?"

"Of course." I bowed my head respectfully. I would never show disrespect to a female, any female. Especially not one who had seen to the happiness of so many of my fellow Coalition fighters.

Warden Egara turned on her heel and left the room. Once gone, the doctor grabbed me by the wrist and held on tightly. "Do not lie to me, Warlord. Is this female your mate?"

That was enough of this bullshit. Between one heartbeat and the next, my beast grabbed the Prillon by the neck and lifted him until his toes dangled off the ground. "Think I lie?" The deep rumbling voice seemed to assure the doctor somehow.

His shoulders slumped and I saw the first glimmer of fire in his eyes. "No. Had to be sure."

The beast set the Prillon warrior back on his feet. "Armor." We were going to war and no fucking way were we going to transport naked.

"Follow me, Warlord. Follow me."

———

STEFANI

I HEARD his voice before I saw him. Standing up, I smoothed out the wrinkles of my blue jeans the best I could. Did I look my best? No.

Would my mate care? Hell no. He was a beast. I could probably be covered head to toe in slime and mud and he would still want to—

Oh. My. God.

A monster wearing Velik's face walked into the room. I'd

never seen him with clothes on. I nearly laughed at myself over my jittery, nervous reaction. He was fierce, covered head to toe in black and gray Coalition armor. He had weapons strapped all over his body, so many I didn't bother trying to count. His weight caused his boots to hit the floor with a thud only a beast could make.

He was intimidating as hell. Still gorgeous. I inspected his face as he approached me, making sure he didn't have anything visibly wrong with him. I wasn't expecting him to look injured. The ReGen pods worked miracles. I knew that. But I'd brought them the jellyfish and spent the next two days literally sick with worry. Worse, the stupid alien doctor hadn't let me see him. Velik had been unconscious inside the pod anyway, so I'd obeyed the doctor's wishes and not argued.

Now, I wish I had.

Velik walked directly to me and stopped three paces away. He faced me, but there was nothing in his eyes I recognized. No heat. No despair or pain. No need. Nothing.

"Velik?"

"My lady." His voice was the right voice. But...

"How are you? I was worried."

He inclined his head as if I were a visiting diplomat, not the woman he'd fucked senseless in the back of a car in broad daylight. "I am well. The doctors tell me I am mission ready."

"Mission ready? What does that mean?"

"Warlord Velik is a valued member of the Coalition's most elite force. His commanding officer has requested his assistance on a top priority mission. We leave within the hour." Doctor Mersan, the Prillon whose face I'd come to hate, offered the information like he was reading from a card, not breaking my heart. He turned to Warden Egara, who I just now realized had followed them into the room. "Satisfied?"

What was he talking about?

Warden Egara looked from the doctor to Velik. She watched him for what felt like forever as I stood frozen as ice. A statue. What was I supposed to do? Why was Velik acting this way? Was it the mission? This all-important mission?

"When will you be back?" I could wait for him. He was mine. It would suck, but I understood a soldier's duty. My uncle had come and gone on more tours of duty than I cared to remember. Then he'd joined the Coalition Fleet and disappeared. I knew a few military wives. It was part of loving a warrior. Part of who Velik was. I would wait and be here for him when he came home.

"I do not know," Velik responded at the same time as the doctor.

"Undetermined."

"Very well, Doctor. Warlord. You should go." Warden Egara's sigh made my chest feel like an elephant had stepped on me. I couldn't breathe.

Velik inclined his head to me, then the warden, and turned as if he were going to leave without even saying goodbye. No good-bye hug? A kiss? If he had an hour, we could do even more...

He took one step and I ran. I threw myself at his body and wrapped my arms around his waist. "Velik. I don't understand. Why are you acting this way? I'm your mate. Don't you remember?"

Silence filled the room, heavy and full of cold dread. Or maybe the ice I was feeling was in my veins. Something was wrong. Very wrong.

Velik looked down at me with a kind expression on his

face. One he might give to a puppy, or a two-year-old clinging to his leg, not his mate.

He lifted one hand and ran gentle fingertips over my cheek. "Apologies, my lady. You are beautiful, but I do not know you. You are not my mate."

7

*S**tefani, Twelve Weeks Later*

NOT FOR THE FIRST TIME, I was grateful for the numb emptiness that filled me.

I pulled up to the guard's station and faked a smile at Rowan, the Elite Hunter who seemed to be permanently camped here.

"Hey, Rowan. Warden Egara is expecting me."

"Sending another message to Atlan? Or are you going to visit your mother again?" He was kind and friendly, so I answered him.

"Sending a message."

"Very well, my lady. Be well." He opened the barrier so I could drive my new SUV through to the parking area. My old car? Gone. Couldn't keep it. Hurt too much.

I went through the paces. Parked. Checked in. Waited for the warden to come out of the black hole of offices and other rooms in the huge complex, and escort me to one of the private rooms used for off-world communication. Adrian and I made the trip at least once a month to talk to our mother, who was living on Atlan. But today, I wasn't calling my mother.

I was calling *him.*

The asshole.

The only beast I'd been able to discover, who, through all of Atlan's history—and I'd looked—had ever... *ever...*refused his known mate.

"Stefani. It's so good to see you." Warden Egara gave me a warm hug and I tried to return the sentiment. Couldn't do it. Not today. "I have the comm room all set up for you. We can call your mom whenever you're ready."

"I'm not here to talk to my mother."

Warden Egara looked confused, but she nodded and led the way to the small room I'd come to know well. Small, round table surrounded by six padded chairs. A large screen on one wall as well as smaller, individual screens that popped up from the table in front of each chair if you wanted to talk up close and personal, more one-on-one than conference style.

I entered the room behind her and she moved to the control station built next to one of the six chairs. "All right. If we aren't calling your mother, who are we calling?"

A huge lump clogged my throat, like I'd tried to swallow an entire loaf of bread whole. Rather than try to talk, I reached into the pocket of my suit jacket—I'd bought the suit special so I would look professional, mature and strong for this—and pulled out a piece of plastic.

Warden Egara watched me with a curious look on her face until I placed the object flat on the table and removed my hand.

"Two pink lines for pregnant, right?"

"Oh my god." Her eyes rounded with shock—or maybe horror—as she looked from the home pregnancy test up to my face. "You're pregnant?"

"Yes. Apparently. Had the ultrasound yesterday."

"I see. And the father—"

"They're Velik's." I hadn't slept with anyone for months before, and none after. So, yeah. That asshole Atlan beast was the baby-daddy. I debated telling him at all, but then I'd remembered what it had been like for me and Adrian growing up without a father. Scratch that, with a father who paid my mother off to make sure he never had to see us. I didn't want that for my children.

"They?"

"Twins. Runs in the family." I shrugged and ignored the dark well of pain-rising up to choke me. Again. Of course I would get pregnant with twins. I couldn't just fuck up one poor infant's life, I had to make it two.

"I—"

I'd never seen her at a loss for words. "You can order genetic testing if you don't believe me. I don't really care if you believe me or not. The only reason I'm here at all is because I'm not the kind of person who is going to keep the children from their father just because he didn't want to be with me."

She sat in the chair, staring at her hands for several minutes while I waited for her to decide what she was going to do.

"Stefani, I'm sorry I didn't believe you. Please, have a seat." She pulled the back of the chair next to her away from the table so there was room for me. I shook my head.

"No thanks. I need to do this standing up. And on the big screen please."

"Do you want me to leave the room once I get through?"

"No. It's fine. This isn't a social call." It was personal, very, very personal. But not social. There would be no love talk or phone sex or secrets told. This was a courtesy call to the father of my unborn children. If he wanted to make an effort to be part of their lives, so be it. If not? So be it. I was done crying over him. D.O.N.E.

I stood patiently as Warden Egara worked her magic at the controls. A few moments later an image of a stranger in a Coalition Fleet uniform appeared on the large screen at the front of the room. He looked at the two females calling him and scowled at us. "This is Battleship Zeus. State the nature of your call. We are in a comm block. In fact, how did you get through?"

His scowl morphed into outright hostility as other fighters moved around behind him. He was clearly on a spaceship somewhere. The gadgets and gizmos behind him could have come straight out of a sci-fi movie.

Warden Egara entered something into her control panel and scowled right back. She didn't appear to be intimidated in the slightest. Which was good, because I was about to throw up all over this nice, shiny table.

"Check your code screen, sir. Protocol IBPWP-5623. This is Warden Egara from Earth. I need to speak with Warlord Velik. Tell him Stefani Davis, the woman who saved him from the jellyfish poison and whom he later spoke with at the processing center, is also here. She must speak with Warlord Velik. The matter is urgent."

The alien—I assumed he was an alien, even though he looked more human than anything—leaned forward in his seat and read... something. Protocol IB—whatever, I assumed. "Very well. One moment Warden Egara. My apologies for my abrupt tone, my lady."

"I accept your apology. I am aware of the unusual and unexpected nature of this comm."

He inclined his chin once more. "Please do not disconnect your comm while I locate Warlord Velik."

Warden Egara assured him we would wait. A second later the screen turned an oddly translucent swirl of colors, as if we were trying to watch what was happening on the bridge of that ship through swirling soap bubbles.

It was about to happen. Oh, god. I was going to see him again. Velik.

My morning sickness, which could be called morning, afternoon and early evening sickness, squeezed my stomach like a vice. It was so bad even my sister had stopped teasing me about it and started keeping a sleeve of saltine crackers in her purse.

I ran for the S-Gen recycling unit I knew was in the corner of the room and heaved the handful of crackers and ginger ale I'd managed to keep down for breakfast. The purge was followed by a round of dry-heaves that made my stomach feel like it was trying to crawl up and out of my throat. God, dry heaves hurt. And my mother had put up with this for *all nine months?* No wonder Adrian and I didn't have siblings.

"Oh, dear." Warden Egara's voice was sympathetic. I didn't need soft emotions right now. Pity. Empathy. I was barely holding myself together as it was.

I felt, rather than saw, the warden get to her feet to try to help me. Not that she could do anything about my perpetual vomiting.

When I was done, I asked the S-Gen machine for a warm, wet washcloth and a small glass of water. They appeared one after the other and I took both from the small alien machine with gratitude. Spontaneous Matter Generators, also known as S-Gen machines. They were amazing and existed all over Atlan and, I understood, everywhere but Earth. Humans, it seemed, had been judged too barbaric and violent to be trusted with such things.

They weren't wrong. My mother wasn't the only one who had spent more than one night in Snook's fighting pits watching grown men tear each other apart for money. Worse were the assholes on the street who tore each other to pieces for nothing at all.

I wiped my face a bit, took a sip of the water and returned to my place. This time, when the warden indicated the chair, I sat. I was all out of stubborn pride at the moment.

I checked my trusty watch. Five minutes had passed. How long did it take to find someone and get their stupid face in front of one of the comm screens? The aliens seemed to have them literally *everywhere*. Couldn't walk more than a few steps without passing one on Atlan. I doubted the interior of a high-tech spaceship would be any different.

"How long does this normally take? What are they doing?" I asked.

"I don't know. It's never taken this long for me to reach anyone before."

The warden's confession didn't help my stomach settle.

I took another sip of water. Another. The glass was nearly gone when the screen finally began to clear. I took a deep breath, prepared myself to say the words I'd practiced at least a thousand times over the last few days;

Hello, Velik. It is nice to see you. I am reaching out to let you know that I am pregnant with twins and you are their father. I don't expect anything from you, but I wanted to offer you the opportunity to be involved in their lives, if that is your choice. If not, please do not concern yourself. I will take care of them.

Followed by a host of horrible, awkward sign-offs that I would most likely never say out loud. *Thanks for nothing. Enjoy the war. You broke my heart, you asshole. So, yeah, see you never.*

Not exactly smooth, but it was the best I could manage. I'd timed my little speech. Took about twenty-two seconds. Twenty-four if I stumbled. Fewer than fifteen if I talked as fast as the typical teenager these days.

After I told him he was going to be a father, whatever he said or did, he did. No matter what, I was going to stand up, walk out of here and get my shit together. I was going to be a mother. I had things to do.

So why was there a huge hole in my chest? No matter how hard I tried, or how much I cursed myself out when I looked in the mirror, I couldn't stop hoping this was all a big mistake. That Velik would take one look at me on the comm screen, change into his beast and demand to be at my side as fast as the outer space transport system could get him to me.

Stupid? Yes. I knew it. Deep down, I knew that wasn't going to happen. But even deeper, where my heart and soul hid inside a little iron coffin, I still hoped.

Damn it.

"Where is he? The ship, I mean." I asked Warden Egara, but she shrugged.

"I don't know. His location wasn't in the Coalition's system. Must be on a covert op."

Well, that was freaking fantastic.

Didn't matter. Max and Kovo had already assured me— once I lied and told them the babies were the result of a one-night-stand with a human loser I never wanted to see again—that anything the babies or I needed would be provided—without exception. Both warlords were rich as Midas, so I wasn't worried about money. I wasn't too proud to take what they offered. For myself? No. I had managed on my own. But for my children?

I'd grown up poor and vulnerable. I knew the streets of Miami. My girls—or boys—weren't going to ever know what it was like to feel like they were at the mercy of the world, or the whims of the local gang leader. Scared. Vulnerable. Trapped because there was no money and nowhere to go. Out of options.

Not my babies. Not. *Ever.*

I swallowed the last bit of tepid water in my glass and cleared my throat. The image on the screen was suddenly crisp and clear, and lacking one very important component.

"Where is Velik?" I glared at the stranger on the screen. If he'd been screwing around this entire time, while I sat here puking my guts out and worrying about Velik's reaction, I was going to transport to that ship and kick him in his alien ball-sack. Hard. With boots on.

"My lady. Warden Egara." He inclined his head. "I sent the communication request to Warlord Velik and have received a reply."

"And?" What was this guy up to?

"My apologies. I will read it to you, word for word, so I do not make any mistakes."

Read it to me? Where was Velik? Why wasn't he taking this comm call? What the hell was going on out there?

The comm operator cleared his throat. "Warlord Velik is not accepting outside communication at this time."

"Did you tell him Stephani Davis was trying to reach him?" Warden Egara asked.

"Indeed, my lady. I would not break Coalition protocol." The male looked offended.

Warden Egara crossed her arms over her chest and shifted away from the screen until her body met the back of her chair. I, however, leaned forward, every bit of weight on my arms as I tried to keep my head and shoulders from dropping onto the table. My spine seemed to have broken in half.

He wouldn't even talk to me? That's what this was?

Not accepting outside communication?

"Let me get this straight." My knuckles, still wrapped around the water glass, turned white. "You actually spoke to him, told him he had a call from Earth, from me, Stefani Davis, and he just said no? He said he doesn't want to talk to me? He said those words to you?"

"Actually, my lady, I indicated the comm was from both Warden Egara and yourself. The response was delayed, but I read it to you, word for word." He looked contrite, as if even he could not believe the warlord would issue such a cold reply. Or maybe that was just my imagination and he didn't really care one way or the other. Like Velik didn't care, apparently. Couldn't be bothered to accept my phone call. Comm call. Whatever.

Asshole. I was trying to do the right thing here, let him know he was going to be a father—despite the fact that he'd promised me the world, fucked me in public, and then acted like he didn't know me at all.

Ass. Hole. I shouldn't have expected any different. My own father had actually paid off our mother, made her sign a legal document stating she would never try to contact him, nor put his name on the birth certificate.

We still didn't know who he was. Not even a name. Our mother had told us he was unimportant, and now I understood. My own father had signed away his parental rights before my twin sister and I were even born. That had been at his lawyer's insistence as well. Mom had been sixteen, poor, scared and probably feeling like I did right now. So raw and hurt she couldn't even scream.

"Thank you, sir." I stood up, nodded at the helpless alien on the other side of the screen and reached around Warden Egara to push the little lighted button I knew would end this farce of a call.

When the screen was dark once more, I placed a hand on Warden Egara's shoulder. "Thank you, Warden Egara. I would ask that you not speak of this to anyone. Not even my sister. I told both her and my mother that the father was a human so that Kovo and Maxus would not feel the need to get involved."

"That was probably wise. I give you my word." She looked away from me and closed her eyes, as if her own emotions were too volatile to control. "And Stefani, I'm sorry."

"So am I." With every ounce of willpower I possessed, I took my glass over to the S-Gen's recycling container and deliberately, slowly, placed the empty glass inside. "I will go now, so you can get back to work. I'm sure the halls are lined with women impatient to be brides."

I walked out of the room, down the corridors and out of the building before the first tear fell.

When I was far enough away from the processing center to avoid anyone seeing me, I pulled my SUV over to the side of the road and sat there, sobbing. Wracking, heaving sobs that I could neither stop nor control. I put the vehicle in park and reached for a new vomit bag from the stash I kept in the passenger seat for special occasions. Like this one.

There was nothing in my stomach, but that didn't stop my body from trying to empty me of everything. Hurt. Hate. Sadness. Shame. Fear—god, how was I going to raise two half Atlan children?

First my father had walked away with no interest in ever meeting his daughters. Then there was my mom's brother, Uncle Fabian. One military tour after another, he left us for months at a time even though he *knew* he was the only man around to help my mother—his twin sister—and keep us safe. Then one day he joined the coalition and never came back. No calls. No check-ins. Nothing.

My mother tried her best, but that meant she had been gone a lot. Working two, sometimes three jobs to keep a roof over our heads, milk in the refrigerator, macaroni and cheese and peanut butter in the pantry.

My grandmother didn't even try. She had given birth to my mother and Uncle Fabian when she was only fifteen. Later in life she had lung cancer and smoked every damn day until the end. She was a bitter, cold woman full of hate for the world. Sometimes I think maybe subconsciously she wanted...well, she wanted the pain to end.

Now I understood.

No one was coming to save me. Still unwanted. Always a burden. Well..I knew Adrian would drop everything to help me take care of the babies, but she had her own life to live. A mate, a warlord, who actually adored her. Loved her.

Wanted her.

———

I CRIED FOR TWO DAYS, the pain a physical thing that twisted and wrenched my guts from the inside out.

On the third day I took every memory of Velik I had, my hopes and desires and desolation, my feelings of being abandoned by my father, my uncle, my bitter grandmother, my mother moving to another *planet*, my twin so consumed by her mate that she regularly forgot to return my calls, and put them inside the iron coffin I built in my mind when I was a little girl. Everything that hurt me went in there, locked away and buried, like radioactive nuclear waste, buried in a deep, dark pit.

Radiation killed things. Slowly. Painfully.

Thinking about Velik, or my past, or about how uncaring most people I had encountered actually were, would rot me from the inside out. So, I didn't do it. I couldn't afford that. I had to live, really live. For my unborn children, I had to not only survive, but thrive. Create a new life and a new history. For them, if not for myself.

On the fourth day I called my friend Carmen...and started packing.

8

arlord Velik, Sector XXX, Battleship Zeus, Fifteen months into mission

WEIGHED down with weapons and gear, I walked down the ramp of the shuttle and watched the young warlords stomp over to their favorite wall of the ship. They'd posted a board, like school children, and were counting their kills.

I'd stopped counting over a decade ago. Longer, perhaps. It was hard to remember. In fact, it was hard to remember anything—old or new—since that jelly creature on Earth had nearly ended me. Whatever was contained in the jellyfish's poison had done more than damage some nerves, as the doctors claimed. The ReGen pod had healed me, they said. Everything was one hundred percent normal.

No. There was *nothing* fucking normal about my life now.

My beast was gone. I wasn't sure when I truly realized this fact. Oh, I could still shift into beast mode in battle and rip enemies to pieces. But it was me doing the fighting, not my beast. There was no rage to carry me through impossible situations. Outnumbered by Hive Soldiers? I had to force my change. I didn't even have to argue with him about it. It was like the jellyfish had killed my beast and left me behind.

It fucking sucked.

I never realized how much I needed that pain in the ass, growling, grumpy bastard. I was healthy. Mission ready. But half of me was missing. The wild half. The fierce, raging, fearless half. The fucking fun half.

I swung my gear into the S-Gen recyclers and made my way to my personal quarters. In no time at all I was cleaned up, the few scratches I'd received on this raid healed with the ReGen wand I kept in my rooms.

Exhaustion weighed down on every cell in my body, but I didn't want to sleep. Resting was great, it was the dreams that haunted me. Every fucking night. Sorrow. Heart-breaking, soul-crushing agony. It sucked me down like quicksand and buried me alive.

And for what? I had brothers in arms to fight with, drink with. My family, as far as I knew, were safe and secure back home, on Atlan.

So why? What the fuck was wrong with me?

As if I'd summoned the feeling, despair dropped me to my knees. Debilitating. Like nothing I'd ever felt before.

"Fuck!" I brought my arm down on top of the small table where I would take the occasional meal. It cracked in half with a loud boom, followed almost immediately by a disembodied voice coming through my personal comm.

"Warlord Velik, this is medical."

"What the fuck do you want?" I wasn't in the mood.

"Our systems are detecting severe stress on your heart and central nervous system. The doctor has ordered you to report directly to medical bay three."

"What doctor?" I asked, but I already knew the fucking answer.

"Doctor Helion, sir."

The comm went silent, but I knew the intrusive little fucker who had access to my vitals could also track my exact location on the battleship. No. Not just on the ship. Anywhere in Coalition space. I'd had the Intelligence Core's leash around my neck for so long I'd almost forgotten the weight of it. Almost.

For years, the beast had raged at being ordered around like an animal. Now the constant tracking and communication didn't feel like anything at all. A nuisance, nothing more. I was here, taking orders from Helion, because I chose to be, because I didn't have anywhere else to go.

I stood, slowly, my free hand rubbing the ache in my chest without conscious thought. I hurt all the time. Nothing I couldn't handle. Just a slow burn, constant pain.

Maybe that jellyfish had fucked up my system more than the docs wanted to admit. Or tell me.

I paused, expecting the beast to offer some asshole retort. Nothing but silence inside me. Great, gaping emptiness.

Fuck.

No sense putting this off.

I walked into Medical Bay 3 a few minutes later. Doctor Helion stood looking over a data screen with Doctor Mersan. They were wearing medical uniforms, standard green. The color of healers.

They should have been wearing black.

Both Prillon warriors were neck deep in I.C. operations. Both were also ruthless assholes in desperate need of a mate to teach them some manners.

I wasn't holding my breath. The day either one of them

was matched to an Interstellar Bride? Well, as the humans would say, that would be the day their fiery hell turned to ice.

"What do you want with me, doc?" I didn't bother asking where to go, just moved to the examination table closest to them and took a seat.

"Everyone out." Helion gave the order and the room cleared of everyone but him and Doctor Mersan. Interesting. Whatever was about to go down was to be kept secret.

"How are you feeling, Velik?" Helion leaned his hips against the counter behind him and crossed his arms, looking me over from top to bottom.

"Mission ready." As always. Point me in a direction and I'd go kill whatever they wanted me to.

"That's not exactly what Doctor Helion is asking." Doctor Mersan moved closer to me with an injector of some sort in one hand.

"Whatever you're holding, you try to inject me with it, and it will be the last fucking thing you ever do." I'd never much liked this Prillon. Helion I'd developed a grudging respect for. But Mersan? He implanted Hive tech in females' brains. Females. And sent them out to find the enemy. No respect for females. He was destructive, not protective.

Maybe I'd just fucking kill him now and save the universe some trouble.

"Calm down, Warlord." Wisely, he took several steps away from me, not stopping until he was just out of reach. "How are you feeling emotionally? Are you having any problems with your beast?"

His cautious question made the hair on the back of my neck stand on edge. What. The. Fuck. "What do you know about my beast?" I stood, glared at him.

"It's a simple question. How is your beast? The mating

fever? Are you experiencing issues with self-control? Excessive rage?"

If he'd still been around, my beast would have come out to play and threatened the doctor with a violent death. Instead, there was only me. I forced myself to partially transform and played the part, my voice deep and soaked with deadly intent. "What. Do. You. Know?"

Helion stepped between us. "Seen enough?"

"Yes." Doctor Mersan returned to the data monitors, opening and closing files, reports, test results. All mine.

The sight brought another swell of despair welling up from my gut and into my chest. Nothing about the emotion made sense. Nothing. But the feeling hit me like a punch to my gut and I sat back down on the table in silence. If I'd tried to speak, the only sound I would have made was one of pain.

One did not show weakness to either one of these Prillon *healers*. Not ever.

An alarm of some sort sounded and Mersan cursed. "I told you. He needs another dose."

"Dose of what?" I asked.

"Not yet. It could kill him." Helion had walked away from me as well, both doctors now with their backs to me, their full attention on their medical scans.

"If we don't do it now, we might lose him. The suppression dose was supposed to be effective for at least two years. It's only been fifteen months. Look at these intercellular saturation levels. They're too low." Mersan picked up the injector in one hand and lifted his other to the screen, pointing at some data that made no sense to me. "See this? We didn't allow for variation in metabolic breakdown between individuals."

"What did you two do to me?"

They continued their argument, completely ignoring me.

Dangerous. Stupid. Fucking. Idiots.

I transformed into my beast, took two steps and lifted both Prillons by the backs of their heads, their feet frantically swinging toward the wall, the screens, anything that would allow them to fight back.

Fuck that.

Just to make my point, I lifted both arms higher, until both of their pointed fucking Prillon skulls touched the ceiling of the room. "You going to fucking tell me, or should I crush your fucking skulls and ask someone with some manners to review your records?"

"You don't sound like a beast, Velik." Helion's tone was mildly amused. I squeezed hard enough that I knew he'd need some time in a ReGen pod when I was finished with him, until things started to pop and crackle.

"Go ahead. Do it." Helion taunted me with a voice I'd never heard before, a voice that sounded as tired as I felt. Resigned. Absolutely without fear. Did the warrior have anything left inside him? Did he have a fucking soul?

I tossed Mersan—and his fucking injector—to the opposite wall, grunting in satisfaction when his back hit, hard, and he slid to the floor. I pointed at him. "Stay."

If he came at me with that injector, I'd kill him.

Helion I handled with a bit more caution. I turned, carrying him with me, until I could set his ass down on the examination table. I let go and stepped away, my back to their screens, both in sight. "Talk."

One word. Not a request.

Helion sighed. Of course it would be him. Of fucking course.

"Velik, listen to me. You called me, remember? From

Earth? You asked me to send you on a suicide mission. Told me your mating fever was so severe you weren't sure you would survive another week. Do you remember?"

I did. It was hazy, and seemed like a long, long time ago, but I remembered. "I was on the beach. Running."

"Excellent." Helion took the opportunity to lift a hand and rub the back of his neck. I didn't smile, but I wanted to. He deserved that and more.

"Answers, Helion. Now."

"Are you familiar with Warlord Maxus?"

"Yes." What the fuck did he have to do with any of this? "He was on Earth. Found his mate. Moved to Atlan." Like I'd wanted to. Hoped to. Find a mate.

"Yes. But do you remember how he came to be on Earth?" When I shook my head, Helion continued. "He was sent there as part of a Hive scouting unit. He broke their mind control, killed the other members of his unit, and survived, undetected, for months."

"What does this have to do with me?"

"He had mating fever, Velik. His beast was out of control. But something in his Hive integrations allowed him to master his beast, despite the mating fever. He's been working with a team on Atlan to try to perfect the treatment."

"Treatment?"

"Yes. We can halt mating fever. Save lives."

"That's not possible." My response was automatic, but even as I said the words the last fifteen months of my life played through my mind in a stream of memories. No beast. The silence inside me. The emptiness.

Hive technology that suppressed the beast? That cured mating fever? How? How the fuck could they stop something so instinctive, so primal?

And then I knew. No. Beast. Somehow, they'd *killed* my beast.

My face was inches from Helion's between one breath and the next. "Did you kill him? My beast? What the fuck did you do to me?"

"Your beast is still inside you, we just gave you something to help you...maintain control."

"When? When did you give this to me?" The despair rose like a tidal wave of darkness and I realized, for the first time, that it came from me. From my beast. Relief flooded me, knowing he was still in there, somewhere. Buried but alive. But why this growing despair? The pain was suffocating, worse than any injury I'd ever received in battle. I couldn't think when it took hold of me. Could barely breathe.

"On Earth. You were in the ReGen pod, on the brink of death. The beast was fighting the poison in your system. Atlan physiology changed the jellyfish's original poison into something much worse. Your brain was bathed in venom. It was going to kill you."

"So you turned me into your newest experiment." It wasn't a question.

"One way or another, you were dead already. And we needed a test subject we knew was suffering from mating fever. We couldn't risk dosing the others until we knew the effect it would have on you."

"The others?" A flash of movement from the corner of my eye made me turn my head slowly. Doctor Mersan was seated upright, preparing to stand. "You fucking stay there."

The doctor gave me a small salute and leaned back against the wall. I returned my attention to Helion.

"How many?"

"A hundred, give or take. I'm not sure of the current count. Some of them may have died in battle in recent days."

I couldn't believe what I was hearing. I knew Helion spoke the truth.

I stepped away from the Prillon so I wouldn't need to resist the urge to crush his windpipe. How dare he do something like this? To me? To...*her*?

Mate. The beast howled the word inside me. The imagine of a female face rose from the darkness and shocked my system like I'd been hit with a bolt of lightning.

Fuck resisting.

My hand was around Helion's throat as the beast rose within me for the first time in over a year.

"MATE!" His booming shout made both Helion and Mersan flinch. The beast squeezed the tender flesh of Helion's throat, just enough to make him gasp for air. I would have let my beast kill the asshole except I needed information.

"Oh, fuck. Here we go." Mersan stood, despite my beast's warning growl. Guess he figured I couldn't kill two Prillon warriors at the same time.

He was wrong.

"Put him down, Velik. He didn't know."

"Bullshit." I answered him. My beast had relented, allowing me to remove our hand from the doctor's neck. More ReGen time for the doctor. Not that I cared. The beast snorted in agreement. "The female. She said she was mine." I glared at Helion. "You walked me in front of her and allowed me to hurt her? Disavow her? Leave her unprotected?"

"By the time I knew the female existed, we had already administered the serum. It could not be undone. I needed to know the treatment truly worked. Facing a female your beast had claimed as his mate was the ultimate test. The toxins in your brain had erased your memories of her. Without your beast, you would not have taken her as your mate, not for two years, at least. Two years that we needed you fighting in the war." Helion explained their rationale while Mersan shrugged as if it was all...analytical. Data and probabilities.

It was true, I barely remembered meeting her, even now. My beast, however, had no trouble at all. He shoved an image of her into my mind with a howl of rage.

This. This was what he'd been mourning. Grieving. Needing.

She was beautiful. Long dark hair. Gold-green eyes. She was young, but knew what I was, where I was from. She'd been...perfect. There had been a boat with sails. Her vehicle...

My cock hardened for the first time in over a year. The sweet scent of her pussy filled my mind. Her skin. Her hands in my hair as I'd...

Fuck. I'd claimed her. Fucked her. Promised her she would be mine forever.

And then I'd stared at her like a fool, told her I had no idea who she was, and walked away.

"Where is she? Who is protecting her in my absence?"

Helion shrugged. "Not my department. I do not meddle in human affairs."

"What did you tell her?"

"Nothing. She was not yours. No mating cuffs. No claim. You said so yourself. You didn't know who she was."

"Fuck you."

"For what it's worth, Velik, I am truly sorry. I would not have given you the serum had I known you'd found your mate. By the time I knew about her, it was too late. I would have tested it on someone else."

"Lies, Helion. Always more fucking lies. Your words mean nothing."

Turning on my heel, I walked toward the sliding door. The unused injector lay where it had rolled to a halt on the floor next to Doctor Mersan. Slowly, deliberately, I crushed the fucking thing under my boot. When there was nothing but cracked pieces grinding under my heel, I headed for the transport room. I was going to Earth, to find her. Protect her. Claim her. Keep her forever, despite the fact I couldn't remember her name.

My beast—thank the fucking gods he seemed to be alive and well—agreed.

Mine.

9

*S*tefani, Pacific Palisades, California

Two little yellow hats. Two little swimsuits covered in a daisy pattern. Two of the cutest babies ever to exist on this world or any other.

"Stop making goo-goo eyes at my girls and get them in the car. I want to get there before they eat all the cake." Carmen, my housemate and best friend in the universe, put a bottle of ultra-protection, baby *and* coral-reef-safe, sunscreen into her bag. In the hall behind her, Henry wrestled with the umbrella-like beach canopy we would stake down in the sand once the obligatory mingling and chatting had been handled.

"Stefani! The babies are going to be late to their own party!" Carmen's voice echoed from an open door that led into the garage.

"Coming!" I finished buckling Terra into her car seat as

Alena kicked and squirmed in hers. I picked both carriers up by the bulky handles, and hauled them out to the large SUV—aka the "mom-mobile". When we weren't together, Carmen drove a bright red convertible that made her look like a goddess with her tawny skin, wild sense of style, and penchant for wearing a lot—a lot, lot—of large jewelry. She had more bling than the queen of freaking England and no inhibitions about showing it—or her gorgeous curves—to the world.

And Henry? He had developed a love for motorcycles, aviator sunglasses and tight leather. With his tall, lean build, sandy blond hair and dimpled grin, all he had to do was come to a stop and single women flocked to him like bees to honey. He was one of the most decent, caring, honorable men I'd ever met in my life. I didn't tell his dates any of that. Up to him. If he wanted to act the *bad-boy* part, more power to him. He was damn good at it.

Henry tossed the rest of our stuff in the back and climbed into the passenger seat as Carmen started the engine. I sat in the back, in the middle, sandwiched between two hard plastic car seat bases. I didn't mind. I had a bundle of pure love on either side of me.

Pop song on the radio, I hummed along, content to sit *still* for five minutes.

"I thought your eightieth birthday was last week! Why are you driving like you're ninety?" Henry loved to give Carmen shit when she was driving. I half suspected he was in love with her, period, and would willingly give her... everything. And if that was the case, he hid it well beneath a cheerful smile and smart mouth.

Carmen tapped the dash with long, bright blue and gold striped fingernails. She called them her cat claws.

Meow.

"Don't mess with me. My girls are in the car. Didn't you see the *'Babies on Board'* sticker I put up in the back window?"

"No." Henry twisted around in his seat to look for it, but there was no such sticker. Carmen smiled, her dark gaze locking with mine in the rear view mirror, as Henry searched for the non-existent sticker.

Score: Carmen 1, Henry 0.

"There's no sticker," he mumbled. "I can't believe I fell for that."

"No sticker. That's because I don't want some psycho to follow us home and try to kidnap our girls. I also don't want to get in an accident with them in the car. So, call me granny all you want, 3 miles below the speed limit is my jam today."

Henry laughed as he turned back around in his seat. I placed one hand in each of the babies' car seats to touch them. Their small, chubby fingers wrapped around mine and I melted inside. They were my why. No matter how badly Velik had hurt me, he'd given me the greatest gift anyone ever could.

I leaned back in my seat and let my mind wander. We didn't have far to go. Palm trees, gated communities and model-gorgeous, perfect people jogging or walking their dogs passed by in a stream of nameless faces. I'd looked like those plastic-surgery-perfect women once. Thin, toned body. Skin glowing. Full of energy.

Now I was exhausted with dark circles under my eyes. My midriff was still stretched out and loose from carrying twins. My breasts had not gone back to normal size, despite the fact I had given up trying to breast feed the first week. Firstly, there were two of them. And second? They were half

Atlan. I didn't know how much a normal Atlan infant ate, but my girls could put away food like nobody's business. How they weren't gigantic rolls of dough, with green-gold eyes blinking out from the center, was beyond me.

The area we lived in was expensive, but stunning. The weather was amazing every single day. And, as required for Henry's current and future happiness, there were ample opportunities to go sailing. Henry and Carmen still sailed at least once a month. For me, gliding across the water had lost its appeal since...

No. Stop that thought right there. Don't think about *him.* At least that's what I told myself at least ten times a day. Which, all things considered, was a fantastic number, down from several hundred.

"We're here!" Carmen's sing-song voice made me grin. Once we parked, she opened the door on my left and lifted Terra, baby carrier and all, out of the SUV.

On my right, Henry did the same, lifting Alena clear of the vehicle.

They headed inside the club house, my girls in tow, both rear doors of the SUV hanging wide open. I unbuckled, laughed, crawled out on one side, closed the door and made a circuit around the SUV to close the other. I opened the hatch in back and grabbed the bag I had packed with baby essentials. Diapers. Wipes. Bottles. Extra outfits. Soft, chew-able toys —they were in the stage where everything went in the mouth, a few small snacks and jars of food. Baby spoons. Blankets. I hadn't weighed the bag, but it was heavy enough to make my shoulders ache if I had to carry it for more than a few minutes.

I looked at the rest of the stuff. Umbrella canopy. Towels. Beach bag. Water bottles.

Nope. Not gonna make it in one go. I would have to make two trips.

Carrying the baby bag that weighed more than my hiking gear, backpack included, I turned to walk inside when Carmen and Henry both emerged from the double doors of the beach club's private entrance.

My Atlan brother-in-law, Kovo, had insisted on paying the exorbitant membership fee once my tattletale of a twin mentioned how much I loved—or used to love—the water. The beach. Sailing.

Used to. Now I had two girls who might die from a single jellyfish sting.

Maybe not, but I wasn't going to risk Velik's children having a reaction to them like he had. Swimming pools and dry land, that was all my daughters were going to get.

I hurried inside despite knowing what I would see. The twins were already out of their car seats, giggling and grabbing hair, glasses, anything they could reach, as a handful of our friends passed the girls around like dolls.

Cute dolls. Happy dolls. I dropped the baby bag on the floor next to the door and joined them.

"There she is! Is that your momma?" Samantha, their closest neighbor, held Terra as she reached toward me with chubby baby arms. Then...she smiled.

I died inside. A good death, love exploding inside me like a bomb had gone off. Good, but still painful somehow. I had this reaction at least once a day. The feeling was magnificent, and it hurt like hell.

God, I loved her. And her sister. Not just loved, *loved*. Soul-melting, raging, gentle, provide a violent death to anyone who even looked at them sideways, loved.

I had to admit, Carmen's idea to throw a party every

month until the girls turned one — instead of taking formal portraits —was a great one. I picked out my favorite pictures each month and those were the ones that got framed and hung on the wall. Today they had turned six months old. I'd moved here a year ago, already three months pregnant. The blink of an eye. And an eternity.

Everyone seemed to be enjoying themselves, young and old alike. After about fifteen minutes we opened a large set of doors that led to an enclosed pool area. A few steps beyond that? The beach. The waves. Perfection. It was a gorgeous day.

Henry took off to meet his sailing friends. Carmen was strolling up and down the beach, sandals in one hand, hanging from their straps.

"Look Stefani! She likes to kick!" Two teenage girls I'd become fond of were holding my girls, wading with them in the shallow end of the water, giggling as the twins splashed and kicked. Alena, especially, had taken to the water like a fish. Fearless. Which meant when she got old enough to crawl, I would have to watch her every millisecond.

I sat on the edge of a sturdy lounger, in the shade, and kept my eye on them as I sipped at a glass of iced tea. I'd brought the baby bag outside with me, just in case. That thing was never more than a few feet from my side anytime we were out of the house.

My cell phone rang. Damn it. I wasn't in the mood to talk to anyone. And who called on a Saturday anyway? Everyone in my personal circle had their own, unique ringer. This was straight up *ring...ring...ring...*

I ignored it. Probably a telemarketer. Or robocall.

Ring...ring...ring...

Annoyed, I dug through the bag and pulled out my

phone. The caller ID showed a blocked number. Ugh. I ignored it and put it back in my bag.

Ring...ring...ring...

"You'd better answer that dear, might be an emergency." The voice came from a kindly neighbor who had successfully raised five children as a single mom. Alone. Like me. She was probably right.

I grabbed the phone. "Hello?"

"Oh, thank god! Stefani? Is that you?"

"Yes." That voice sounded familiar... "Who is this?"

"It's Warden Egara, from the Brides' Processing center in Miami."

Something twisted deep down in my gut.

"Do you remember me?"

Did I remember the only witness to the bleakest moment in my entire life? "Yes. I remember."

"I'm sorry. I'm not sure how to tell you this."

"Tell me what?" My gaze locked on my daughters, my anxiety rising. Had the Atlan government somehow found out about them? Were they demanding the twins go to Atlan? Or was it our government demanding they be sent away because they were hybrid alien children? Every nightmare scenario I'd envisioned—and there had been a lot of them—flashed through my head in the blink of an eye.

"He's here."

"Who?"

"Velik."

Oh god. Nightmare scenario numero uno; Velik wakes up one day, finds out about the twins, decides he wants them after all, and comes to Earth to take them away from me. Not fucking happening.

"Stefani? Did you hear me?"

"I heard you." I was already throwing things back into

my bag as quickly as possible. Sunscreen. Baby hats. I stood up and yanked the towel off the chair I'd been sitting on. I had to get out of here. Take the twins home. If that asshole thought he was going to waltz up after all this time and take my girls, he could rot in hell. I had an Atlan stepfather and brother-in-law who would help me put Velik in the ground. Especially once they learned the truth.

"Stefani?"

"What?" I motioned with my arms for the teenage girls to bring the twins back to me. Shock had been transformed into fear. That fear was now becoming something else. Something vicious, protective and in a fucking hurry to get out of here.

How had he found out? I'd tried to tell him about the babies, but he wouldn't even talk to me when I called him on his stupid spaceship. So, why now? Why fucking now?

Didn't matter.

So what if Velik was on Earth? Miami was the only transport pad I knew of on the North American continent. He wouldn't have flown a spaceship to get here. Earth was too far away. So, he must have transported to Miami. He still had to cross the country to get to us. A non-stop flight from Miami to LAX took just under six hours.

"Stefani."

Jesus. Christ. "What? I'm a little busy here." I would call Adrian on the drive home. Get her husband—mate—whatever—Kovo, ready to roll. "Thanks for the warning. I need to go."

"But—"

I pressed disconnect and tossed the phone into the baby bag. I asked the teenagers to get the twins dried off and buckled into their car seats. I said there was a family emergency, and no questions were asked. The teenagers headed inside, my neighbor going with them to supervise.

Perfect.

I grabbed the baby bag and walked down to the sand. Carmen was too far away to hear me shout, so I lifted my hand to my mouth and let out a shrill whistle. She turned around and hustled back toward the clubhouse.

I couldn't stand still. I was too anxious. Nervous. My mom-rage had soured into panic. I walked out onto the sand and met her halfway.

"What's going on?"

"We have to go."

She titled her head and looked at me, really looked. As usual, she had no trouble reading the room. "What's wrong?"

"We have to get out of here. I need to take the girls home, like right now."

"Okay." She did the balancing thing where she wobbled a bit as she lifted first one foot, then the other to slip her sandals back on. "I got that part."

My sigh felt like it traveled from the soles of my feet to get to my lips. "Their father is here. He's coming to take them away from me."

"What? He wants to take them to Atlan?"

Of course, she knew the truth. Of freaking course. I'd been lying to myself thinking I had fooled her for even one moment.

Score: Carmen 2, Stefani and Henry both stuck at 0.

"Yes. No." I bit my bottom lip. Let go. "I don't know, okay?"

"I thought he didn't know about them. That you—you know—and then he disappeared."

"I went to the processing center when I was three

months pregnant and called the battleship where he was stationed."

"You did? Holy shit, Stef. Why didn't you tell me? What did he say?"

"He refused to speak to me."

For the first time I could recall, Carmen looked like she'd been shocked speechless. "He *refused* to speak to you?"

"Yes."

"And he knew it was you calling?"

"Yes."

"That mother-fucker, son-of-a-bitch. I'm going to kill that giant, alien asshole with my bare hands." She grabbed my hand and pulled me along at a fast clip, on board now with getting the hell out of here. "I thought Atlans were supposed to be super protective and really good to their mates? You know, like Kovo and Max. Those two are amazing. Don't you dare tell Adrian, but I'm jealous as hell."

"Me, too." Or at least I had been, once upon a time. I was finished with daydreams and fantasy. No one was going to come sweep me off my feet and be eternally devoted to me. I'd accepted it. Didn't like it, but I had other things to worry about now. First and foremost, two small, vulnerable people who relied on me to keep them safe.

"I *knew* we should have forced you to put Henry on their birth certificates."

"What?"

"You should have married one of us. God, it's too late now."

"You both knew?"

"Duh. You, Stefani Davis, are a terrible liar." Carmen stopped tugging on my hand as we entered the beach house. "Don't kill the messenger, but your sister and your mom know, too."

"Why did I even bother?" I'd been feeling guilty about keeping my family—Carmen and Henry included—in the dark all this time—and they knew? They *all* knew?

"We figured it helped you cope."

"You discussed this?"

"Of course."

"When Adrian came out to visit, Kovo was—"

"He doesn't know." Carmen lifted one baby carrier—I smiled at Alena as her car seat swung around to rest against Carmen's side. "Neither does Max."

That made more sense. Kovo had held the twins and cooed at them, sung them Atlan lullabies until I was forced to either leave the room, or break down in a crying fit.

Should have been Velik doing those things. *Shoulda, woulda, coulda...*

Carmen smiled at the two eager teens. "Thanks ladies. You are both super helpful." They blushed and scurried away like bashful mice. I thanked my neighbor, and she followed the teens back out to the pool.

I lifted Terra, safely buckled into her car seat, and we walked out front to the parking lot so we could drive home.

Speaking of home... "What about Henry?"

"Don't worry. I'll text him." Carmen waved off my concern. "He can use a ride app or get a taxi. He's a big boy. He'll figure it out."

We locked the car seats into place and then climbed into the front seats.

Ring...ring...ring

"Shit." I had to twist myself into a pretzel to dig around inside the baby bag. I'd left it on the floorboard behind the driver's seat. I pulled it out, sat up straight and cursed again. Same blocked number. "Warden Egara."

"Well, answer it." Carmen accelerated out of the parking lot like we were in a drag race.

"Hello?"

"And find out *exactly* where he is. We need to know how much time we have." Carmen whisper-shouted the instructions as Warden Egara's voice came through loud and clear.

"Stefani. Don't hang up."

"Not going to. Sorry about that. I was surprised, that's all."

I heard the warden sigh and waited to find out what she needed to tell me. Then I would find out exactly where Velik was. Maybe he wasn't here for the twins at all.

But then, why would the warden be calling me?

"I called to let you know Warlord Velik is here, on Earth."

"Yes, thank you. I got that. What I don't know is why."

"I don't know what happened between you two, or how the hell he walked out of here like he did." She paused, muttered something under her breath that sounded like helium? Like, for balloons? Huh?

"I don't understand. Why did you call me? Why is he back in Miami?"

"He's not in Miami. He's in California."

"What?!" *Shit. Shit. Shit.* I turned to Carmen and mouthed the words, 'he's here', while pointing down toward the ground.

Carmen didn't say a word, but the back of my head hit the headrest as the SUV jolted forward.

"Warlord Velik contacted your father."

"I don't have a father."

"Under Atlan law, Warlord Maxus is your father and protector. Upon his death, should you still be unclaimed, your brother, Warlord Kovo will take over as your legal protector."

"So? This is Earth, not Atlan. I don't really care about their laws."

"Well, you should. Warlord Velik has claimed you as his mate. Warlord Maxus gave him your address on Earth."

No. This wasn't funny anymore. "When?"

"About twelve hours ago."

10

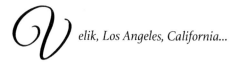

elik, Los Angeles, California...

HUMAN MEANS of travel had to be the worst in the Coalition of Planets. My knees hit the back of the seat in front of me, the car smelled like something called pachouli—at least that's what was written on the exterior of the offensive package and the human male driving the vehicle repeatedly looked back and forth from me to the road.

"You play football?"

"I do not." I knew the competitive game some of the larger males of Earth liked to engage in. I had watched one such battle on the humans' television.

No one died. And the males were...small. Once was enough.

"Basketball, right? You play for the Lakers?"

"I do not." Another human competition of running and throwing ball through a hoop for points. Again...the fighting pits on Atlan or the Colony were of much greater interest.

However, as Earth did not have access to ReGen technology, I could understand the non-aggressive nature of their sporting events.

"Okay, okay. I'll stop asking. They made you sign an NDA. Am I right?"

"Yes." I had no idea what this *NDA* might be, but I would agree to anything at this point if it made the young male stop speaking to me and drive. Faster. "How long until we reach the home of Stefani Davis?"

"I don't know who lives at this address, but we're almost there."

"Excellent." I had waited too long already to claim my mate, to kneel before her as she locked the mating cuffs around my wrists. I would never leave her side again, would devote myself to her happiness. Her pleasure.

Mine. The beast rumbled just below the surface. I forced him to remain quiet, grateful for the additional control I still had. Helion's serum had not left me completely. Not yet.

The human driver smelled of anxiety and fear. Should the beast appear, he would likely lose control of the vehicle and delay my arrival.

"You know, this is a hoity-toity area, right? You gotta know somebody to get past the guards."

Guards? I approved. Even human guardians were better than none. Although, on second thought, ReCon teams that fought in the Hive war had recently added human fighters. They were vicious, quick and highly adaptable. Adding Earth's fighters to the fleet had helped regain some territory from the Hive. Something we had not managed for several decades.

"Here we go. If we can't get through, I'm going to have to drop you off here."

"That will do."

"It's a two mile hike up the hills to this address."

Two miles. "That is nothing."

"Okay man, if you say so." He shook his head and turned up the noise coming from the primitive sound devices built into the shell of the car. Some music. Some humans speaking. All irrelevant.

Now that I was close to my mate's home, I inspected the area. The smell of the ocean was inescapable. I wondered if the deadly jellyfish creatures lived in these waters as well.

Tall palm trees and large plants, covered with blooming flowers, filled every space and were nestled between human buildings. I had lived in Florida, on the processing center's grounds, long enough to become familiar with many human customs and devices. This place, California, was not much different. Black tar and concrete roads. Primitive and inefficient vehicles polluted their atmosphere. Humans without homes meandered everywhere, most covered in dirt, starving, ignored by others. Even human children. It was a disgrace.

I did not understand this world. I did not want to settle here. I wanted to go home, to Atlan. Show Stefani the beauty of the central gardens. Our oceans were dangerous places filled with large predators, but our beaches were lovely. I knew she liked the water. She left one home near an ocean to another.

I wanted to take my mate home. Yet, I would live where Stefani desired. She was my home now.

"Here we go." The driver stopped the vehicle in front of a large metal gate that blocked the tar road. He lowered his window. In the center of the area stood a small building. Two males in uniform watched our approach. One of them walked to the car window with some type of board in his hands.

"Name?"

"Look man, I'm just his ride." My driver looked over his shoulder at me. "What's your name?"

"Velik."

"Velik what? That a first name or last name?" The guard leaned down so he could look me over.

"It is my only name."

"A real comedian?" The guard shook his head. I inspected him in turn. He was large, for a human, but I could crush him easily enough. He was armed only with a short stick of some kind and a device I knew to be capable of shooting electric current through its victims.

First time I'd seen one, the other guards and I had purchased some of the weapons and spent an entire evening shooting one another while drinking Atlan wine. I had been stung by the ineffective devices many, many times.

"I am not a comedian." A human occupation. Not mine.

My driver snorted, as if my words amused him. Perhaps I needed to clarify further.

"I do not play for the Lakers or compete in human football."

The guard mumbled something to himself about drugs. "All right, wise guy, what's the address?"

The driver told him. The guard flipped through some documents and looked at me. "Velik?"

"Yes."

"Sorry bud, your name isn't on the list."

"Of course not. She does not know I am here."

The guard chuckled but his expression seemed to imply that I lacked intelligence. My driver shrank, appearing to be shorter in his seat. "You need to turn around and go home. People around here don't like unexpected guests."

"Sorry about this." The driver apologized to the guard, not to me.

A loud siren sound blared from multiple places. The car's speakers. The comm device that my driver used to navigate to Stefani's home. The guard also had a comm device in his pocket. He pulled it out, read something on the screen, and cursed.

It appeared to be some sort of human warning system.

The loud siren stopped. The voice on the car speakers changed.

This is a code red alert for residents of the greater Los Angeles area. A shelter in place order is in effect. Authorities are looking for a white male, seven-foot-three, three hundred pounds, dark hair, mid-thirties. The suspect is wearing a black t-shirt, pants and black boots. He is considered armed and extremely dangerous. Last seen at LAX. Reportedly heading toward Pacific Palisades. If you see the suspect, call 9-1-1 immediately. Do not engage. Repeat...

The voice repeated the exact same information.

I shrugged. Human criminals were not my concern. The male in question sounded to be large for a human but would pose no threat to me or my beast.

I opened the car door and exited the small vehicle, grateful to no longer be in such tight quarters. The moment I did so, the vehicle tires squealed as the car raced backward, leaving me behind. Which was fine. The driver had warned me I might need to walk from here.

The gate was no impediment when on foot. Fuck that, it was not even close to secure. I could bend it in half with my bare hands.

Ignoring the two human guards, I took three steps toward a grassy area that would bypass the gate.

"Hold it right there."

I turned to find the human males both pointed their electrical weapons at me.

"Don't move." The guard who had not spoken before held his comm device to the side of his head. He was speaking to someone, telling them the name of the street where we stood. His name. The name of the neighborhood that had been etched into the large stone someone had placed on the corner.

Were we to reside here, that stone would need to be removed. The gate would also need to be improved. This was not secure. Not even close.

Perhaps I could hire a group of Elite Hunters to replace these ineffective human males. Nothing so pathetic and weak as these humans would guard the entrance to my mate's home.

A revving engine approached. A much larger vehicle by the sound. Beyond that, police sirens, additional sirens adding to the discordant total each minute I stood, looking at the guards.

The male nearest me shook. Definitely needed to find some Everians for the job. When the male did not speak again, I turned and resumed my walk.

The sharp pain of two little stingers pierced my back. I recognized the bite of the electrical weapon. I sighed.

I did not want to kill the humans. The beast, however, would not allow them to keep us from our mate. Just like the officers at the airport who had insisted I stay in their interrogation room once I walked off their aircraft. I had no need for any of these idiots. Were I not connected to the small human by wires, I could have kept walking, just as I had at the airport.

I turned around, wrapped one hand around the wires connecting me to the small weapon, and yanked the stingers from my flesh. The angle was not the best. I would need to use a ReGen wand on my back. Or not. The wounds were small.

I would allow my mate to tend me. She would decide.

I tossed the wires back toward the guard.

"Fuck!" the guard yelled. His friend fired his weapon at me. This time the stingers hit me in the chest.

That was it. I tried not to kill them. They insisted.

Two steps. The front end of a large vehicle skidded to a stop, mere inches from my hip. The warmth of the engine radiated toward me. The heat irritated my beast almost as much as the stench of the fuel it burned.

With a growl, I jerked the stingers from my chest and threw them on the ground. My beast roared a warning.

I heard the door of the vehicle open, but my beast had focused on the guard, on removing his head.

"Velik! Stop!"

My mate's voice invaded my body. My cock hardened. The sound of my own heartbeat became thunder in my ears. The urge to kill shifted to lust. Need.

I turned to find her running toward me. Instead of throwing herself in my arms—as I had hoped—she grabbed one arm and tugged. "Come on! Jesus. Every time, you're in trouble."

"I am not in danger. They are no threat." I growled at the guards, somewhat hurt and offended that my mate thought so little of my skill. Both of them stumbled backward, one landing on his ass and scooting away like a frightened child. "I will kill them quickly. Then I will claim you, mate."

"You're not killing anyone. God." She pulled as hard as she could. I relented, needing to please her more than I needed to kill the inept and foolish human males. "Hurry up! The cops are going to be here any minute."

"I do not fear humans."

"No kidding. Just shut up and get in the car."

I allowed her to pull me along, my beast pleased to have her hands on us. Her scent drove me—us—to distraction. Every breath made my cock harder, my need stronger.

Fuck. Claim. Mine!

I told the beast to fuck off. He was not helping. This was not the place.

She was ours. Soon, I promised him. Soon our cock would be buried deep, her cries of pleasure would reach our ears. The taste of her sweet pussy would coat our lips. We would touch every part of her, kiss her everywhere. Make her come over and over as her pussy clamped down on our hard cock.

Stefani led me to her vehicle, a large SUV. She shoved at my shoulders until I sat in the passenger seat. I looked over to find a female I recognized behind the wheel.

"Carmen."

"Asshole."

That was not my name, but I would not correct Stefani's friend.

My mate attempted to close the door. I slammed an open palm into the plastic casing.

"What now?" Stefani looked over her shoulder as if afraid. The sound of the human police sirens grew louder.

"Not without you."

"I'll get in back."

"No."

"Shit." She looked over the top of the vehicle at the two guards who watched. They lived because they had not approached my female. "We were never here. You hear me? He ran off when you called the cops, and you have no idea where he was going. He ran that way." Stefani pointed in the opposite direction of her home. "Understand?"

When they were silent, she cursed again. "If the cops show up at my house, I'm going to turn him loose on you. You'll be dead in a day. Understand me? *Never. Here.*"

The guard who shot me in the back nodded. "Just get him out of here."

"Open the gate," Stefani ordered.

Both guards walked inside their small structure. The black gate rolled away from the center on small wheels I had not noticed earlier.

Stefani stood next to my door and inspected the situation inside the vehicle. There was nowhere for her to be but in my arms.

My beast approved. Our mate was protecting us. Fighting for us. And soon she would be ours, safe and protected. An excellent beginning.

Stefani climbed into the vehicle and settled her bottom on my thighs. Her back pressed to my chest. I wrapped my arms around her as gently as I could manage with my beast roaring inside me. It was a good thing she was very small. I barely fit inside the vehicle, and she had to bend her head toward my neck to avoid bumping her head on the ceiling. My beast purred, the despair I'd felt for so long lifting as her soft body pressed into mine. She sat there, in my lap, where she belonged. Where she would always belong.

"Hurry up. Close the door." Carmen, the young female who had been with Stefani the day I found her, issued the order. I obeyed, and the SUV shot past the gate toward my mate's home at a speed the humans would consider illegal.

I approved.

In my arms, Stefani's soft curves stiffened as if she were trying to separate us again. Pull away

"What are you doing here, Velik?"

"I am here to claim you, Stefani. You are my mate."

"Right. I've heard that line before." The disdain in her voice set off warning bells in my mind. Those warning bells became full alarm at her next words. "You shouldn't have come."

11

WE DID NOT SPEAK AGAIN until the vehicle was securely inside a parking garage. The moment the vehicle stopped, Stefani opened the door and bolted from my lap.

I tried to tell my beast not to be hurt at her rejection, but he had fought so long, so hard. Despair rose within me once more. I told the beast to knock it off. We simply needed to woo her. Pleasure her. She was ours.

I exited the vehicle and closed the door gently, not wishing to agitate my female any more than she already appeared to be.

A large rectangular object moved from where it hung inside the parking garage, suspended and parallel with the ceiling, to stand upright, creating an enclosed space. I had seen these before but never been inside one. Restricted to the processing center grounds, my experience with such things was limited. Not completely secure, it would have to do for now. Stefani was walking away from me. Carmen slipped from the driver's side and watched Stefani, a question I did not understand on her face.

Stefani looked from me to Carmen to the vehicle, then back to Carmen. "Don't forget to text Henry. I'll take Velik upstairs so we can talk, if you'll take care of unloading the...car?"

"Of course." Carmen looked over her shoulder, as if inspecting the contents of the vehicle, a look of concern on her face.

"I offer my assistance." No female needed to lift or unload anything in my presence. Ever. Especially if the physical labor caused concern.

"No!" Carmen closed her door, her movements even more tentative than mine had been, the locking mechanism barely audible as it clicked into place. Perhaps Stefani was even more fragile than I had thought. "It's nap time, you know? I'm really tired. And most of this is my stuff. I'll just take everything to my room."

"Okay. Thanks." Stefani agreed instantly and walked into her home. Curious about her private quarters, I inclined my head to Carmen and followed my mate. She offered brief descriptions of her home as she went, waving her hand at each area we passed. "That hallway goes to the suites. That's the living room. The kitchen. There is a pool outside. That's the family room."

Every step took us farther from Carmen and closer to privacy. Her home was large and well kept. I was glad she had been taken care of in my absence. Still, I had trouble focusing on her words. My gaze remained glued to the feminine sway of her hips as she moved. Her ass was perfect, even fuller than I remembered. I wanted to hold each side in one hand as I fucked her, held her back pressed to the wall, thrust deep. Skin on skin. I wanted her hands in my hair, pulling me closer, demanding more as I licked her pussy, worked her clit. Made her scream.

My memory of taking her was hazy. Incomplete. I needed her. Now.

My cock ached, the pain more intense with each step. By the gods, she was too fucking beautiful. Her long hair hung like silk, perfect for holding her in place as I fucked her. Every curve enticed me. Round. Perfect. Her body was softer than I recalled, her breasts larger. Everything about her seemed to be enhanced, more feminine, just...*more*.

Perhaps that was my beast and his raging hunger to taste her. Perhaps it was true memory, and her body had changed shape. I didn't care. She was mine. She was beautiful. I simply *needed*.

"My suite is down here. I have a private salon where we can talk."

The sound of Carmen moving around the home barely registered as my mate invited me into her private quarters.

"Just a sec. It's kinda messy." Stefani indicated I should wait. Pleased that she would fuss over the appearance of her room, I indulged her. My beast was pleased as well, happy that she wished to impress us.

I waited in the doorway as she hurried to and fro, picking up items until she held a small heap that she promptly tossed into a connected room.

What she carried, I did not know. Truthfully, I hadn't paid attention. My gaze lingered on her ass. Her breasts. Her lips. The pair of pants she wore stopped mid-thigh, revealing long, shapely legs and smooth skin.

I would kiss those legs. Caress the inside of her thigh with my lips and tongue before I tasted her. I would have her bare, one thigh on either side of my face, her wet pussy open for me to play with until she came all over my tongue.

Uncomfortable, I adjusted my cock and tried to remain patient. To please her. To do what she asked and needed me to do so she would feel comfortable and safe. So she would accept us, honor us, find us worthy.

Her collection of items gone, she closed the connected door and locked it. I grinned. I did not need to inspect any items that embarrassed her, nor did I care about her collection of shoes or clothing.

In fact, I would gladly keep her naked so there would be no need of such things.

"Okay. Come in." She stood with her back to the door she had locked, her breasts clearly outlined by the thin material of the shirt stretched tightly across them. There were buttons.

I would bite them off with my teeth.

"Velik?"

Fuck. I'd been staring. I forced myself to move slowly so as not to startle her. I walked into her private sanctuary and locked the door behind me. To my left, a bed more than big enough for both of us taunted me.

I needed her. Velik, the man. I would lay her down and spend hours pleasuring her in that bed.

But the beast *needed* her even more.

"Come in. The salon is over here." She turned her back to the beast and moved to another room.

Fuck.

Mistake.

I couldn't control him. I couldn't stop him. He fucking refused to listen, done with me and all the long months spent away from our mate. He viewed those months as a complete and total failure on my part. He was correct. I had abandoned our mate. He had not. In fact, he had fought and clawed to return to her.

I had forgotten she existed. Serum or no serum, I should have known...

In the blink of an eye, my failure, my shame, was buried beneath the beast. He tore the shirt from his chest and dropped it on the floor as he followed her.

Skin to skin. That was what he needed. Craved. Would die without.

Mine.

The beast was built for battle, fierce but silent when he chose to be. We moved into the room behind her. Stepped closer. Closer. Until the heat of her body crossed the slight distance between us.

"Velik." Stefani spun around. She collided with my bare chest.

The beast wrapped her in his arms and pulled her to him. "Mine."

She pushed at his chest, but her attempt was half-hearted. After a few seconds she stilled, her forehead resting against me. "Why are you doing this? Why are you here?"

"Mine."

"That's what you said last time. Then you left. Looked me in the eye, said you didn't know who I was, and left me." The scent of her tears drove the beast insane. I argued with him, insisted he wait until we could explain.

The beast knew only one way to woo his mate. Pleasure. And only one thing he would die to provide; protection. Those were the only two things he understood.

"Well?" she demanded. She lifted her chin and looked my beast in the eye.

"Stefani." The beast lifted one hand to caress the side of face. "Prisoner."

"What?"

He leaned down and kissed the tears from her cheeks. Tasted them. Moved lower to kiss her neck. She tilted her head back to give him better access. Accepted his touch. "Stefani. Mine."

"But—"

With a growl that warned me to shut the fuck up and stop interfering, he slipped his hands around to her ass, kneaded the soft mounds and lifted her off her feet.

"Velik. We really need to talk."

"Mine."

I gave up and slipped away, became one with the beast until there wasn't him and me. Just us. Me. *Mine.*

I lifted her and nudged her knees wide. When she complied, I placed her pussy over my cock and rubbed our bodies together, our clothing the only thing separating my cock from her wet heat. I tilted her body until she shuddered, a soft moan escaping her throat as her clit slid up and down my hard length. She was wet and ready for me, her cream called to me with a sweet scent that made me shudder. Tightness, compression, a slight twinge of pain and I knew my cock was coated with pre-cum. For her. Everything I had, everything I was, my very life, belonged to her.

"Need you. Mine."

She wrapped her arms around my neck and leaned back in my arms to look up at me as I moved her up and down over my cock. "Why do you have to be so hot?"

I purred, pleased with my mate's admiration. I was strong. I would protect. I would pleasure. I would be hers. Only hers.

"We really do need to—"

I took her lips, claimed her. Devoured her taste with an urgency I couldn't fight, more than a year of repressed lust surging to the fore. Hunger. I could not get enough. Needed more.

There. The bittersweet agony I remembered as she buried her hands in my hair and pulled me closer. Desperate. Needy. My mate demanded more.

"Mine." The one word nearly a roar, I set her on her feet. I removed my clothing in seconds. She watched me, her gaze taking me in from head to toe. Her attention lingered on a new scar. Rested on my cock.

It strained to reach her.

I dropped to my knees and closed my teeth over the top button holding the fabric closed over her breasts. *Mine. My breasts.*

She gasped but did not stop me. Her shirt gone, I inspected the sling she used to support her breasts. I saw no buttons. Fuck. I had to get in there.

I pulled the two straps from the top of her shoulders down to her elbows, lowered the top of the thick fabric until her flesh spilled out the top.

A groan filled the room. Deep. Needy. *Mine.*

They were soft. Full. Bigger than before. I remember the pink covering she'd worn before, the white shirt I'd torn. Her breasts had grown larger.

Gods. She was going to fucking kill me.

I kissed them because I had to. Sucked first one, then the other nipple deep into my mouth. Tasted the peaked nipples, rolled my tongue over and around them, again and again. Pulled as much of the soft mound as I could into my mouth as she guided me, her hands tight fists in my hair.

Still feasting, I pulled her short pants over her hips, down to her feet. Small undergarments remained. I quickly rid her of those as well. Mouth still locked over one breast, I lifted one ankle free of the clothing and set her foot father away from her body. Legs spread open.

I filled my left hand with the softness of her ass. My right I slid from ankle to calf. Calf to back of her knee. Knee to outer thigh. She was small. I had no trouble sliding my hand over her hip, down her soft bottom to the opening between her legs.

I tilted her hips with my left hand, slipped a finger from my right deep into her pussy.

"Velik!" My name exploded from her lips. I smiled around the mouthful of soft breast, popped the nipple free and clamped down on the opposite side as I fucked her with my finger.

One finger. Wet. Deep.

Two.

She went wild when I pulled back on her nipples, as much of her soft mound inside my mouth as I could get. I sucked on her entire breast. Pulled it inside me. Deep. Throat deep.

Moved my fingers in. Out. Wiggled them until she moaned. Slipped my fingertips around and around the sensitive opening until she shuddered, her knees giving way.

Of course I caught her. Held her. She was mine.

Her hands fluttered as if she fought for control. She moved them to my shoulders, her fingernails clawing at my skin like a wild cat's.

I pushed deeper into her core, rubbed the tip of her womb with my fingertip, my mouth a hungry, pulsing beast feasting on her breast.

Her release came hard and fast, her pussy clamped down on my fingers. Her nails dug into my shoulders, locking me in place. I growled, unable to contain my joy. She wouldn't let us go. Finally, I was home.

Head thrown back, she let out a keening cry I'd never heard before, but would make sure I fucking heard again, every day for the rest of my life.

The beast, I realized, had been letting me play, afraid that if he tried to take her, as he had before, she would refuse him. Us.

Now she was ours. Mindless. Needy.

The beast stood, lifting her easily. She clung to the beast, her pussy pulsing with aftershocks, her body soft and yielding.

Three steps and her back was to the wall. The beast took over completely. Torso holding her in place, he lifted both of her hands over her head and wrapped one of his own around her wrists, locking them in place.

Lifted her hips. Thrust slow. Deep.

Fuuuuck.

Her tight pussy stretched around my cock. Squeezed. So fucking hot. Wet. Tight.

The keening cry I was already addicted to left her throat again. Her pussy pulsed around my cock, her orgasm clamped down on me like a fist. Opened. Closed. Pulsed around me. Tighter. Wetter.

I pushed deeper. Pulled out. Drove her mad. Each time her spasms slowed, I fucked harder. Shifted. Sent her to the brink again. And again.

When she was wrung out, sweaty, sobbing, I stopped moving. Cock buried balls deep, I held utterly, completely still. One. Thing. One, would push me over. Make me come.

I didn't want this to be over. Ever.

"Velik." My name was a plea on her lips. For mercy? For more? Didn't matter. She said my name. Mine.

My orgasm rolled through me, savage and painful. Bliss and agony. I buried my face against her flesh as my seed pumped into her body. Filled her. Marked her. Claimed her. She was mine. Fucking mine. I would kill anyone who tried to separate us again.

I stood still for long moments after it was over. Connected. One. I couldn't give her an inch of space. Not yet.

I released her wrists. She lowered her hands to my head, wrapped her arms around me and shuddered. Skin to skin. I cradled her to me.

She sobbed.

Had I hurt her?

She sobbed again, the sound pure and filled with pain.

With a gentleness I never knew I possessed, I lifted her chin. When her gaze met mine, I cupped her cheek. Gods, she was perfect. A miracle.

Mine.

Tears streamed from her green-gold eyes, a river of emotion on her cheeks.

"God, I hate you, Velik. I fucking hate you."

The words were raw. Brutal. Honest. And I knew she meant every soul crushing word.

12

How long could one hide in a shower? I didn't know how long I'd been standing here, hot water streaming down my back, but my fingertips looked like raisins.

Long enough.

Maybe he'd be gone when I went back into my room.

I snorted at my own stupidity. Not likely.

I was ruined. Sex in the back of my car? Hot. Definitely hot.

But this?

A heart attack had been a legitimate concern. If we were going to stay together, I was going to have to start working out again.

What would happen if he ever got me on my back in a nice, soft bed? Spent some time with his mouth working downtown, like he had in the car?

Another sob threatened to start the ugly train again. I

shoved it down with the determination and grit I'd gained over the last six months of being a single mother. Pregnancy. Nine months of puking my guts out day and night. Pushing not one, but two babies out of my body. Forcing myself to move when I was sore, broken and exhausted from labor every time the twins needed me. Moving when I was literally too tired to remember my own name.

There was exhaustion, and then there was taking care of a newborn. That was next level. The first time in my life I'd actually fallen asleep standing up. If the microwave hadn't beeped, I probably would have fallen over.

And I'd had help. Lots of help. Carmen. Henry. My sister had come for two weeks, my mom for a month after that. By then I'd hired the nanny and things started to settle down a bit. I'd survived.

Sure, I was alive, but heartbroken. Staring, each day, at the two most beautiful faces in the world, wondering what *I'd* done wrong. Why a male from an alien species that was absolutely *legendary* for their devotion to their mates, had not been devoted to me. Spent hours staring at my stretched out, overweight, post-baby body in the mirror, and cried myself to sleep more nights than I cared to remember.

Velik had rejected me when I was thin and fit with a bikini body. When I didn't have dark circles under my eyes and breasts not-yet recovered from swelling to the size of melons.

Every day had been a mental, physical, and emotional battle. But I'd survived. I'd accepted his decision to leave me behind. Grieved. Raged. Hated myself. Hated him. And— finally—acknowledged the absolute *fact* that my girls and I would live our lives without him.

Terra and Alena. One named for the Earth, and one for Atlan. A secret acknowledgment of their father, and one I'd kept to myself, buried deep where no one would examine or question it.

I turned off the water and stepped out to dry off. Hiding was not my style. Never had been. But I was going to cut myself some slack on this one.

I put my hair up in a twist and pulled on the clothes I'd brought in with me. Soft jeans, an even softer sweater that fell past my hips and would hide my post-baby stomach.

Although, he'd just fucked my brains out and touched me like I was the most beautiful woman he'd ever seen.

Lies. He'd made me feel that same way once before. Chosen. Special.

Lies. Lies. Lies. But now he wasn't the only one lying, was he?

The twins. Carmen had taken them to her room. She would keep them there until I gave her the 'all clear'. And maybe, if they didn't have one of their screaming fits and I got Velik out of here, he wouldn't hear one of them.

No. I would tell him, just like I'd tried to that day with Warden Egara. Even if I could never be with him again, I had to tell him. He was their father. As much as he hurt me, I wouldn't hurt my babies. I knew what it was like to grow up unwanted by my father. I would not curse my girls to suffer that same mental gauntlet. The self-doubt. The endless wondering *why? Why? Why?* Hating every Father's Day and every kid in my elementary school class who had a doting dad show up to...well, anything.

"Stefani?" The knock on the door was surprisingly soft, considering the size of the man—alien—doing the knocking.

"Just a minute. I'm almost done."

Kicking myself for calling, but doing it anyway, I put on a

bit of mascara and some blush. Just enough to feel like I looked okay, without looking like I was *trying*.

I rolled my eyes at myself in the mirror. What was this? Junior High?

Turning around, I opened the door. Velik stood there looking exactly the same way he had when I'd grabbed my things and locked myself in the bathroom.

Confused. Hurt. Like if he said the wrong thing to me I'd break.

Maybe I would.

Maybe I already had.

At least I didn't have to worry about getting pregnant again. The doctor had recommended birth control at my six-week checkup and I hadn't argued. Mostly, I didn't want to explain to the nice doctor that the father of my children was an alien who had left me behind a long, long time ago.

"Do you want to take a shower?"

"Sure. Thank you." Velik stepped away from the door so I could exit the bathroom. He walked inside and closed the door. The water was running soon after and I took the opportunity to hustle to the other side of the house and check on Carmen and the twins.

"Carmen? It's me."

The door to her room opened almost instantly. She poked her head into the hallway and looked behind me. "Where is he?"

"In the shower."

"The shower?" She looked me up and down. "You had sex with him, didn't you?"

No use lying. "I couldn't help myself. He's hot as hell, and it's been a while." Sure, that was it. Hormones had over-ruled my head. Totally justified the idiotic decision I'd made to let him touch me. But, holy hell, had he *touched* me.

Carmen pulled me into her room and shut the door. I looked around to see the twins happily rolling around on a blanket, playing with their toys. "So now what? He's back. He is acting all obsessed beast. He is obviously still into you. What are you going to do?"

"I don't know."

"What did he say when you told him about the twins?"

"I didn't. Not yet."

"Shit." Carmen crossed her arms over her stomach like I'd just punched her in the gut. "You're going to get us both beaten to death by a beast."

"He would never hurt a woman."

"He hurt you, didn't he?"

"Not like that. Not physically."

Carmen sighed. "You're right. He didn't hit you. What he did was worse."

I wanted to argue, the need to defend him rising in me without conscious thought. But I couldn't. I'd been punched. Kicked. I'd been in my fair share of catfights in High School. No punch had ever hurt me like he had. Not even close.

"I'll tell him when he gets out of the shower. Right now, I need some girl time." I put a smile in my voice and joined the twins on their blanket. Their happy squeals and coos at seeing me lifted my spirits like nothing else could. I leaned over, taking turns blowing raspberries on their bellies as they shrieked and giggled.

God I loved them. So much.

Carmen walked over and sat down on her bed, watching us with a happy grin on her face.

Neither of us heard the door open.

"Stefani?" Velik's deep voice held more than one question.

Shit. Not exactly the sit-him-down and explain things slowly idea I'd been working on. Too late now.

Still sitting, I twisted around until I could look up at him, my heart pounding. "Velik. Come here. I'd like you to meet your daughters."

He looked from me to the twins, his gaze taking them in, every detail. Their green-gold eyes that were an exact match for mine. Their dark hair. Their happy gurgling as they both tried to wiggle their way over to me.

I watched the expression on his face change from confusion to shock. Then rage. Despair.

Love.

Tears pooled in my eyes as his gaze filled with pure love. It hurt, watching him love them so much, a hard, stabbing pain behind my eyes.

I'd made the right decision. He would be a good father. Whether we were together or not—and I was undecided, despite the hot sex—he would dote on them. Protect them.

Still looking at my handsome warlord, his hair the exact same shade as the girls', I leaned my head to each side, toward each of my daughters as I introduced them to their father. "This is Terra... and Alena. They're twins, Velik. Six months old."

His gaze darted between them. Back to me.

He stepped forward...

I'd never seen an Atlan faint before. But that's exactly what he did. The big, bad Atlan warlord toppled like he was a tree, and I'd swung the axe.

13

*S*tefani, *Three Days Later*

I HAD a book in my lap, but I wasn't reading. I couldn't take my eyes off the gorgeous warlord reading Atlan poetry to his daughters.

A WARLORD MIGHTY, a force to be reckoned,
On the battlefield, his rage beckoned.
His armor heavy, his heart light,
He fought with all his strength and might.

THEY DIDN'T UNDERSTAND a word of it, and I decided that was a very good thing. Their father apparently loved poetry. He was very expressive, voice rising and falling dramatically, hands swinging through the air making wide arcs. He made faces at them as well, playing peek-a-boo over the top of the tablet he'd used to download the alien *literature*.

If I'd known how horrible Atlan writers were, or how bloodthirsty, I would have banned it from my house. Velik, however, insisted that in his native language the words were beautiful, *like his girls*.

When he said shit like that, I let him get away with murder. Well, when it came to the twins. Not with me. I knew he meant all three of us, but I decided to pretend he referred to only two, small, exquisite infants.

He stood a few steps in front of our daughters, a captive audience strapped into their highchairs, eating a snack before their afternoon nap.

Velik walked to Terra first, then Alena, placing a sweet, gentle kiss on top of each girl's head. Then, he leaped back, dropped into a low, exaggerated bow that made Alena laugh —Terra was too busy throwing a cracker on the floor to properly appreciate the theatrics—and lifted the tablet.

"Warlord's Sacrifice. This is a good one.

'CLASH OF WILL, *the scent of blood,*
    Cries of pain, like a raging flood.
    Thundering boots, the pounding drums,
    Battle raged on, death the sums.
    He killed with skill, his enemies fell,
    Their screams and shouts, a living hell.
    The stench of death, a constant reminder,
    Of the cost of war, a solemn binder.

OH, *Mighty Warlord knows the cost,*
    The tears shed, the souls lost.

Battle never won without a price,
He carries that burden, a sacrifice.
For the mate he loves,"'

HE PAUSED DRAMATICALLY and lifted his gaze to lock with mine as he finished.

"'HE FIGHTS. He dies.
Only in death,
Forced to leave her side."'

SUBTLE. Luckily, his last dramatic flourish had sent Alena into a squealing fit that wouldn't stop until her father took her out of her highchair. Both girls were a mess, a handful of snacks smeared across each of their trays, their faces and in their hair.

Not to be outdone, Terra joined her sister, matching scream for scream. It was a game they played sometimes, just like the mumbling twin-speak I heard developing more and more in their interactions. I had no doubt they would have their own language worked out before their first birthdays.

Adrian and I *still* remembered noises and movements we'd used to communicate when we were young, things no one else on the planet would understand. That shared life, being a twin, was something I held sacred. I was beyond grateful that my girls would share that as well.

Velik cursed, his large hands wrestling overlong with the plastic snaps and buckles that held the twins in place. But he persisted. Soon he had a little one in each arm, both of his daughters reaching for his nose as he turned his face back and forth between them.

"You're my beauty." He turned. "And you're my beauty." He looked at daughter number one. "Smart, perfect girl." Back to the other. "Smart perfect girl."

His voice was...goofy. The sound shocking, coming from a male warrior over seven feet tall.

"Do we want to read some more?" he asked them.

"No."

"No."

Carmen and I answered in unison. We'd been listening to poems about mighty warlords killing things for an hour.

Velik chuckled, also odd. His satisfied smile somehow even more adorable than it had been yesterday. He was more and more perfect every day. He was becoming extremely difficult to resist.

"Then we will sing instead." He returned to his back and forth communication with the infants in his arms. "What song do my girls want to hear?"

He left the kitchen to walk up and down the long halls. His voice rose, a deep baritone that many opera stars would kill for. His tone was smooth as silk. Deep. Sexy. Gentle. The way he looked, singing lullabies to my—our—babies? Sweet songs about love and protection and family?

More tears. They filled my eyes, burned like fire water.

Shit. I hadn't been this much of an emotional wreck— not counting the whole *You're-not-my-mate-I've-never-seen-you-before* thing—since right after I gave birth and the hormone swing, combined with exhaustion, threatened to ruin me. One day I'd cried for almost an hour because I couldn't find a particular pair of shoes. Insanity.

Carmen sat down opposite me in one of our cream colored chairs and raised a brow. Velik had wandered to the far end of the hall, where he would make the turn and come back to the kitchen. Repeat.

"What are you doing?" Her whispered words sounded more like an accusation than a question.

"What are you talking about?" I whispered back.

"Him." She swung her hand, half eaten sandwich and all, in Velik's general direction. "What are you doing with *him*? Are you being deliberately cruel? Or are you really this stupid?"

Her words landed like a boot in my gut. Only a best friend, or a sister, could get away with saying something like that. Carmen wasn't my blood sister, but she was as good as.

"I'm not being mean. I want the twins to know their father."

"That won't work. It's all or nothing. I told you. All. Or. Nothing."

"I don't believe that."

"You haven't done your homework."

I hissed. "Watching Bachelor Beast on T.V. is not *doing my homework*."

"What about Henry?"

"What about him?" He was most likely sleeping over at his latest cover model girlfriend's apartment until Velik was gone. "Did you text him?"

"Yes." Carmen shrugged with an –uh, huh, you are so totally freaking delusional—look and shoved the rest of her sandwich into her mouth.

Good. If her mouth was full of turkey and lettuce, she couldn't badger me.

Velik and the twins were getting closer, too close for me to have this argument with Carmen—again. A man could be a fine father without being in a relationship with their mother. I'd seen it play out with some of my friends from school whose parents had divorced. Carmen thought I should forgive him, have non-stop sex, and move to Atlan— where there were no jellyfish.

Part of me wanted to. A big part of me. But the other part of me, the part that had broken and cried at his betrayal, the part that had hoped and made the *leap,* had *trusted* him when I'd learned early in life not to trust people—especially men—just couldn't jump off that cliff again. I hadn't touched him since the orgasm festival that first day. He slept on the floor in front of my bedroom door. I offered him a spare room. The couch. Anything.

He refused. Which was endearing and aggravating at the same time. I told him he could sleep in the babies' room. He refused again, stating that would leave me unprotected. *Me.*

I didn't want him focused on me. I had agreed to let him stay here for a couple weeks, but not for myself. Since the fiasco in my bedroom, where I'd lost control and had sex with him—again—I had very carefully and deliberately avoided any kind of serious discussion. I loved him. I wasn't such an idiot that I would lie to myself with him right here in front of me. I loved him, but I didn't trust him not to vanish on me. Walk away. He claimed I was his mate, that we would be together *forever.*

I'd heard that line before. Less than two days later he'd walked up to me in front of multiple people, looked me in the eye, and claimed he didn't have any idea who I was.

His goddamn sperm had probably been working its way into my fertile little egg at the very moment he denied he knew me at all.

Some things were hard to forgive. After he'd refused to accept my comm call out in space? Nail in the forgiveness coffin. He'd hurt me so badly, I'd felt dead inside by the time I had stopped crying. Actually *dead*. Cold. Numb.

I never wanted to feel that kind of pain again.

Carmen hopped to her feet with a bit too much energy. I scowled at her. She grinned, mouthed the words '*Talk to him*' and called out for Velik to bring the twins to her.

"Nap time!"

Velik handed the twins to Carmen without argument, his gaze locked on me the entire time.

Oh, God.

Guess we were going to have that *talk* whether I was ready or not.

But not here. Not in the house where our daughters slept and either Carmen or Henry—who I hadn't seen in three days—could interrupt us at any moment.

The door to the girls' nursery slammed closed just a bit too loudly.

Thanks, Carmen.

Velik didn't miss the message either. I stood up and he was there, so close that half a step would have me pressed to his warmth, his strength.

Which I could *not* depend on. Remember that.

"Stefani. Mate."

"Don't start with that. Let's start with the reason you looked me in the eye and lied."

"I have never lied to you."

My *humph* came all the way from my bones. "You looked me dead in the eye and told me you didn't know who I was. And I quote, '*Apologies, my lady. You are beautiful, but I do not know you. You are not my mate.*'" I matched his cadence and apologetic tone perfectly. Wasn't difficult. I'd played that moment over and over in my mind thousands of times. Every single one of them hurt.

"Please. Let me explain."

"Go for it. Explain to me how your beast could claim me

as his, have sex with me—in my car, in a parking lot, for God's sake—and *forget who I was* a day later."

He reached for me, his hand grazing my hip as he tried to pull me into his arms.

I jumped away as if burned. I couldn't have this conversation and let him touch me. I was holding on by a thread as it was. If he held me close, like I mattered to him, I would lose it. Scream. Fall apart. Cry for days. Just…no.

Head bowed, he knelt before me like he was proposing, or waiting for me to tap his shoulder with a sword. Neither of those things was going to happen.

"Stefani, I beg your forgiveness. The jellyfish poison attacked my mind. The doctor said the ReGen pod rebuilt the cells in my brain as quickly as they were being destroyed, but my most recent memories were lost."

What? Agitated and upset as much for what he had suffered as for myself, I paced. Thinking. Viciously squashing the little ray of hope that fought its way out of the black tar pit that was Velik's corner of my heart.

"What about your beast? It's not your memory that makes an Atlan claim a mate. It's his beast. Did your beast have his mating instincts—or whatever it is—destroyed, too?"

"No. But—"

"No? So where was *he* when you told them you didn't know me? When you literally said I *wasn't* your mate?"

Still on one knee, he reached toward me again.

The front door opened. Henry walked in. He dropped his gym bag on the floor and took in the scene. "What the fuck is he still doing here?"

Velik rose to his feet.

Henry moved quickly, placed his body between me and Velik.

Was he crazy?

"Move, human. Or I will kill you."

"Fuck off, you piece of shit. Do you have any idea what you put her through? No. You don't. You weren't there, holding her while she cried herself to sleep every night. For *weeks*. Taking her to baby classes so she wouldn't feel anxious about bringing our girls home."

Our girls?

Velik fought the beast, I could see the struggle for control as the bones in his face shifted from normal to—beastly—and back again. "I recognize you, human. You were with Stefani when I found her."

"I was. I have been. I've been here for her, taking care of her, after you destroyed her." The vehemence in Henry's voice was shocking. And I realized the truth.

It wasn't Carmen that Henry was secretly in love with. It was me.

"Henry—"

He whirled around to face me. The stark truth was there, in his eyes. "Tell him to fuck off. Marry me. I swear I can make you happy. I'll make our girls happy. I can protect you. Let me take care of you."

"Mine!" The deep growl made Henry turn. But instead of moving out of the way, as I expected, he dropped into a fighting stance.

"No! Don't hurt him!" I meant to stop Velik from hurting Henry.

Henry snarled. "He deserves some pain."

Velik lunged. I screamed, expecting bones to crack, Henry to go flying through the air.

Instead, it was Velik who flew, his body slamming into the ground a few steps away. His gaze locked with mine and I saw Velik, the rational man, fighting for control. Henry wasn't dead because Velik knew I wouldn't be pleased. He'd heard me.

Henry, however, seemed to want a fight. I knew he was strong, for a human. At just over six feet tall, he was almost exactly a head shorter than Velik. But he didn't transform into an eight foot tall monster, a warlord whose entire society held battle in such high esteem they wrote never-ending songs and poetry about it. Henry should have been terrified.

He wasn't. He didn't move, watched as Velik got to his feet slowly, every move controlled. Deliberate. Velik was holding the beast in check, barely. For me. Only for me.

"Henry, stop. Leave him alone."

Henry's focus was complete. Intense. For him, no one but Velik was in the room. "Yeah? Big boy? You think you're a beast? I've been *waiting* for you to show up." Henry slammed his hands into his chest and yelled every bit as loudly as Velik had. "Come on! You don't deserve her, you piece of shit."

Someone had to make this stop. Nothing made sense. Henry was going to get hurt.

Carmen's voice broke through my confusion. "Henry's been learning that krav maga stuff for years. Once you got pregnant, he added boxing and weightlifting." She was leaning against the wall just inside the entrance to the hall, arms crossed over her chest. Watching. Uncon-cerned. "I did ask if you were being cruel, or just stupid."

"What?"

"Stupid, then."

She hadn't been talking about Velik? But about Henry? Or both?

What the hell? Was that where Henry disappeared to for

hours on end almost every night? I thought he'd been out on dates, drinking whisky and seducing women.

He'd been boxing? So he could fight Velik? For me? He truly believed he could fight an Atlan and *win*?

Was everyone in this house insane?

elik

You don't deserve her, you piece of shit.

This human male was in love with my mate.

Wished to claim her as his own.

My beast was enraged. Ready to kill. *Wanted* to eliminate the threat.

Don't hurt him! Stefani's plea played over and over in my mind, orbiting my thoughts like a bright star I could not ignore. I could not hurt this male.

Henry. Human. He vowed to protect my mate. Claim her as his own. His face held no fear when his gaze locked with mine. He was strong, for a human. The look in his eyes one I had come to recognize among the human fighters in the Coalition Fleet. Determination. Stubborn will. They adapted quickly, were deadly and effective in close quarters – where a beast's size became a weakness.

Reluctant respect filled me as I took his measure. He was not a beast, but he would be a strong and devoted mate.

I did not blame Stefani for his devotion. I understood the desperate look in his eyes all too well. He loved her, as I did. Would kill to protect her, as I would.

He had not failed her. He had not failed our daughters.

I could not kill him. Stefani would be hurt if I injured this male. Should I fail in my efforts to claim her, he would remain at her side.

"Henry, don't. Please." Stefani pulled on his arm until he looked down into her eyes. In an instant his aggression turned to gentleness and he pulled Stefani to his side.

I watched her melt into his embrace. She wrapped her arms around him and allowed him to hold her.

As she would not allow me.

Pain engulfed me. My mate had chosen. So be it.

I moved past Carmen and walked down the hall to the babies' room. Quietly, so as not to disturb their sleep, I stepped inside. They were beautiful and perfect, like their mother. My death would have meaning now, knowing they existed. They would grow into intelligent, worthy females, protected and nurtured.

I was not the first beast to face this path, nor would I be the last.

Still, I had not expected the pain to slice like a blade of ice through my chest. Shockingly brutal. Agonizing.

This was what I had done to Stefani. This was the pain she had felt, facing my rejection.

Such a thing did not deserve to be forgiven. I should never have asked.

I said a small blessing over my daughters and touched their softness a final time, my fingers lingering on the sweet innocence of each little face. Faces I would never see again.

"Velik?"

I turned to find Stefani watching me. "I did not injure Henry."

"I know. I didn't think you had."

Satisfied with her acceptance of my word, I leaned down over the wall of each cradle in turn and kissed my daughters one last time.

When I stood, Stefani held out her hand. "Come on. We need to finish our conversation."

We left the room, then the house. Stefani drove the SUV to a parking area similar to the one where I'd claimed her. The smell of salt water and fish, the sounds of crashing waves, greeted us as we left the vehicle behind and began to walk.

I followed where she led until we walked side by side on the beach, the surf washing up a few steps shy of my feet.

"Don't go in the water. There are jellyfish in California, too."

I nodded in agreement and kept pace next to her. She would speak and I would respond. I had no right to ask for more than that.

"We were interrupted. If your beast wasn't hurt by the poison, why didn't he just claim me again when he woke up?"

"He did not awaken, my lady." The proper address rolled off my tongue, part of my respect for her wishes. She was not mine. I had no right to be so familiar.

"Why not?"

"My mating fever was severe. I was days from death when I found you."

"What?"

"My mating fever was severe. I was days from—"

"I heard you the first time." She rubbed her upper arms

with both hands, as if trying to bring warmth to her skin. I removed my shirt and draped it over her.

"Thanks."

"It is my honor."

"Why are you talking to me like that?" She turned to look at me, gasped at the sight of my bare chest, and turned to face forward. "Never mind. So, your fever was really bad. You were going to die. And then what?"

"I ran, long distances and often. The physical fatigue helped me control him. But even that was no longer helping." I stopped walking and turned to stare out over the water. The size and scope of such a thing inspired awe, made me feel calmer about my future. "I stopped that day and stared at the water for a long time. I knew my time was over. I placed a comm call to my former commander, a Prillon warrior named Helion."

"Did you say Helium?"

I turned and looked down into the delicate features of her upturned face. "No. His name is Helion. He is the commander of the Intelligence Core as well as a doctor."

When she didn't ask anything else, I continued. "When a beast is lost to mating fever, there are two options. Either he returns to Atlan for execution, or he requests an assignment that will insure an honorable death in battle. I requested such a mission. I also told Helion that I would not last much longer. Days perhaps."

"That's terrible."

"It is our way."

"I know. My sister and my mother are both mated to Atlans. I know about mating fever and the executions. It's still terrible."

"It is merely biology."

She turned away from me to look out over the water

herself. "Okay. So, you called the doctor. Told him to send you on a suicide mission."

"Then I heard your voice."

"I was on a sailboat a quarter mile from shore."

"I heard your voice, my lady. My beast recognized you immediately. First, he tried to go directly to you, through the water."

"So that's how you got all those jellyfish stings."

"They were nothing to me. You were the only thing that mattered. When I realized I could not move quickly enough to reach you through the water, I ran."

"Yeah, you did." She grinned. "Carmen and I watched you run. She said you were chasing the boat. I didn't believe her."

"I was not chasing the boat, I was chasing you."

"Okay. I know what happened next. Skip to the part where your beast didn't know who I was."

"He never forgot. He fought every day to return to you."

"Then why didn't you?"

"Doctor Helion and some others were working on a new treatment. Your father, Warlord Maxus, managed to control his beast for an impossible amount of time, and break the Hive's hold on his mind. The doctors discovered something unique in his blood, something new. They studied it and created an experimental serum."

"Max? As in my stepfather Max?" She lifted a hand to rub at her forehead as if she were in pain. "I went to Atlan. I was even in that prison, hospital, whatever you guys call it. That's where we were when Adrian found Kovo. I met the doctor working on Max's blood. They said it would help warlords control their beasts."

"They needed to test the serum on a beast they knew was on the edge of death. The poison in my system was another reason they chose me. I was dead one way or another. They gave me the treatment before I regained consciousness. When I transported from Earth, I didn't know they'd done anything to me."

"What did they do to you?"

"They silenced my beast. Completely. He was raging, and then he was gone."

"This is so messed up." She took my hand in hers, the act small, but a gift I would never forget. "So, the poison erased your memory and the doctors put your beast to sleep. But why didn't you talk to me when I sent the comm to your ship?"

I stilled inside, every cell quiet and alert. "There was no comm."

"Oh yes, there was. I went to the bride center to call you. I was pregnant. Even though you didn't remember who I was, I wasn't going to keep you from being a father."

"You did not contact me."

Her voice rose in tone and grew louder with her rising anger. "Yes. I did. I went down to that stupid place, plastered a fake smile on my face for Rowan so I could get in, showed my pregnancy test to Warden Egara, and we put a comm through to you—wherever you were. Somewhere out in space. On a ship. Warden Egara said the only way she could get access to you at all was because of some IBPWP—something. It ended with numbers."

"Interstellar Brides' Program Warden Protocol. The numbers represent the planet and processing center where the comm originates. It is a way for our mates to contact us in extreme emergencies, no matter where we are."

"Well, you didn't want to be contacted. The guy running the comm on the ship said you were not accepting outside communication. From anyone." She took a deep breath and blurted out the last. "Not even me."

Not accepting outside communication?

That was a standard response, sent in the event any fighter in the fleet received a message when he was not on the ship. Some operations required stealth. The Hive had managed to intercept communications in the past, troop locations, operational details. When Helion sent out a secret team, no one was told when we left, nor when we returned.

And if anyone tried to contact one of us?

Gods be damned. Fuck. All of this. Stefani's pain. The time lost. All because I'd been deployed on a secret operation, and not on the ship, when she tried to reach me.

It was as if the gods themselves schemed against us.

She had done all things honorable and right. She had accepted my beast and welcomed his claim as soon as we'd met. She saved my life, rushing me to a ReGen pod, when I'd been weak and unconscious from the poison in my system. She had remained at the center, waited for me to waken, to reunite with me. Make my claim official.

I had rejected and abandoned her after claiming her body and promising her everything. Still, when she discovered she was carrying my child—our daughters—she had reached out across space and time to find me. To tell me the truth and invite me to be part of their lives.

Never had I known of a female treated so poorly, respond with greater strength or honor.

I had rejected her, hurt her, and denied her at every turn. By my own hand or another's, I was not worthy of her.

I had never been worthy.

Turning to face her, I gently held the hand she had gifted to me and lifted the other to her face. "You are a female of worth, Stefani Davis. I cannot imagine what you have suffered. There are no words to express my remorse. You deserve so much more than I have given you."

There they were again, shimmering in her eyes. Tears. Proof of the pain she suffered at my hand.

No more.

"I understand now. I do. I just need time." Her quiet voice trembled. I leaned down, unable to deny myself this one fucking selfish moment, and kissed her. I was gentle. Reverent. She was divine. A goddess. A spectacular and powerful female.

"I will return to Miami today. I will give you time, my Stefani. All that you need. I will cause you no more pain. I cannot bear it."

She nodded and leaned into my hand. "Thank you for understanding."

"Anything you need, I shall provide. Right now, you need time to heal."

"Yes."

I kissed her once more when she dropped me off at the airport. I avoided LAX and the annoying police stationed there. Stefani placed a call to her sister, mate of Warlord Kovo, and said something about the FBI.

A private plane waited to take me back to Miami.

Once there, I used the processing center's comms to contact my family on Atlan. I left very specific instructions for them regarding my daughters, who I hoped, one day, they might have a chance to meet.

That done, I summoned Kovo and Adrian to a meeting. Elite Hunter Rowan volunteered to assist me. He left the processing center and returned soon after with Stefani's sister, Adrian Davis, and her mate.

"Why are we here, Velik?" Warlord Kovo approached me first, his mate safely blocked from my view. I approved of

Kovo's caution. I was an unmated male known to have mating fever. Had my beast raged, I would have killed anything and everything in my path. Male or female. Animal. Once the beast lost control, nothing stopped his killing frenzy but death.

Adrian's presence was a painful shock to my system, her appearance nearly identical to Stefani's. Twins. Their likeness was uncanny. Except this female did not have the same dark, silken hair. Nor did she have my mate's generous curves.

Adrian was beautiful, but she was nothing compared to her sister.

I lifted the ornate box I carried and held it out to Adrian. She looked at Kovo, confused. "What is that?"

"This contains various records and seals detailing my wishes regarding my Atlan properties."

Kovo glared at me. "Why are you giving such a thing to my mate?"

"I am entrusting both of you to see that my daughters' estates are maintained until they come of age. You are their only Atlan family on Earth."

"Why aren't you doing it yourself?" Adrian's softly spoken question didn't stop her from accepting the ornate box. I'd asked the item be transported from the home I'd grown up in. The box was decorated with our family crest and had belonged to my grandmother. Inside were my mating cuffs, coded to my wealth and property. It pleased me to think that my daughters would have it.

"*Your* daughters?" Kovo's voice deepened. "*You* are their father?"

He might have attacked had Adrian not placed her hand on his arm. I knew the power of that small touch. Appreciated its intensity even more due to my lack. No mate. No mating cuffs around my wrists. I tried not to stare at the cuffs Adrian wore. It would be too easy to imagine them on her twin. On Stefani.

He did not try to kill me, but his disgust was clearly evident. "You claimed Stefani and then abandoned her? You are not worthy. No warlord dishonors his mate in such a way."

"I agree." I met his angry glare with acceptance. No one could hate me more than I hated myself for what I had done to my mate. No one. "I entrust my daughters' estates to you. Stefani will own everything, of course, but I do not wish to burden her with oversight when she does not wish to live on Atlan. She has chosen another. A human."

I looked from Velik to Adrian. "Perhaps your father would agree to assist you." I spoke of Warlord Maxus. By Atlan law, he became Stefani's and Adrian's father when he took their mother, Vivian, as his mate.

"He will."

"Thank you." I turned to leave them standing in the middle of the parking lot outside the processing center. The sun had long since set but the air remained heated and heavy. Muggy, the humans called it. Clever, as it indeed felt as if the air itself were attacking.

"Where are you going?" Adrian asked, her voice so similar to Stefani's that I nearly stumbled.

"Helion has been saving a mission for me."

"Helion?" Adrian's tone was far from friendly. "Don't even get me started with that guy."

"It is due to Helion that I am alive and with you, mate. Do not forget that," Kovo teased.

"Yeah, well, I like the results, but his methods suck."

I nodded at her apt observation. Apparently, she knew the doctor well.

"Gods protect you, warlord." Kovo said the familiar words, giving them their proper weight. I'd heard them more times than I could remember. I'd spoken them to others as well. Too many times.

A blessing spoken to a warlord who would not be returning from battle.

15

I MISSED him so much it hurt.

Even Terra and Alena, and their ridiculous cuteness overload, didn't stop my heart from aching.

All I did was ask for a little time. That was smart and reasonable. Right? Velik's story was one of the craziest things I'd ever heard. Our relationship a calamity of bad timing and even worse luck.

God, I'd only known him for a few days. Like, seriously. I'd spent a couple hours with him the day we met, and one of those hours had been frantically driving his unconscious body to the doctor.

The other hour had been magical and given me my girls. But still, it was two hours.

Then five minutes when he'd broken my heart right before he left the planet.

I saw him again, Carmen nearly hits him with the car,

and less than an hour later he's taking me against the wall and I'm sobbing his name.

Then, I'm just sobbing.

Two bouts of hot sex, three days of watching him fall in love with his daughters, and one sad conversation on the beach.

What did that add up to? Love? That was just stupid. When he was here, the thought crossed my mind that I was in love with him. But how could I be? I was in love with the *idea* of an Atlan beast. Real love didn't work that fast. Did it?

"You going to stare out the window all day?" Carmen sipped a cup of coffee and stared at me in my wrinkled pajamas and puffy rabbit socks. She was dressed for work and, as usual, looked like she'd stepped off the pages of a fashion magazine. "Nana said that's all you did yesterday. All. Day."

Nana was the nanny we'd found. She was an older widow with lots of baby experience. Her own children had moved across the country. And yes, she was more than old enough to be the twins' grandmother. Besides, Nana was easier than Margaret. Or Mrs. Westerhall.

She was with the girls while I sat here wondering how it was possible to miss someone I barely knew.

"Earth to Stefani? Are you going to sit here all day?"

"I don't know." I spoke the truth as I knew it. "Henry moved out last night."

"I know." She didn't say another word. She didn't need to. Henry had shown his hand, laid everything on the line for me, for the twins. When he'd asked me, again, to marry him? Tried to kiss me?

All I'd been able to think about was Velik.

Henry kissed me on the forehead and walked away. I

cried, but I couldn't ask him to stay, not when I knew I would never love him the way he deserved to be loved.

The way I loved Velik and my girls. With all my heart. Oh god, there it was. I swiped a tear off my face. I loved Velik. Not an idea. An Atlan.

This was stupid. I was going to call him. Today. Tell him I'd thought things over and wanted to try again. Start over. I'd asked for time and he'd given it to me. I'd known it was a mistake when I'd dropped him at the airport and drove away.

I was stubborn. And stupid. Carmen had called it. Stupid about Henry. Stupid about Velik. Stupid to keep lying to myself. I wanted Velik and he wanted me. Sometimes shit happened and it sucked. Sometimes people got hurt. No, not sometimes. All the time. I was tired of being afraid. Maybe I'd get my heart broken again. If I did, I'd survive. I knew that now. I would cry and then I would get on with my life.

Forget tonight. I was going to call him now.

I waited as the phone rang on the other end. When I got Velik's voicemail, I hung up and sent a text.

Call me. I miss you.

My cell phone buzzed less than a minute later. In a rush of fumbling fingers, I checked the message. Not Velik. Adrian.

We're at LAX. Be there in an hour.

Adrian was in L.A.?

"What's that look?" I'd completely forgotten that Carmen was still standing there, sipping her black coffee and watching me.

"Adrian and Kovo are on their way."

"Nice." Carmen and Adrian were good friends as well. "Girls' night! When are they flying in?"

I shook my head. "No. They are already here. Adrian said they're at the airport and will be here in an hour."

"Guess you better get dressed then." Carmen wiggled her eyebrows at me and left for work. The roar of her convertible's engine speeding down the street made me smile.

Some things changed, and some things didn't.

I checked my phone every couple minutes.

Velik didn't respond to my text. Maybe he was mad at me now.

An hour later I was standing outside on the front step, showered, dressed and waiting, when Adrian's and Kovo's rental car pulled up. Adrian jumped out and ran into my arms.

"Twin," she said.

"God, I missed you." I hugged her tightly. My sister was here, which generally meant I could fall apart if I wanted to.

I did, but I was so tired of crying and second-guessing everything I said or did. I was wrung out.

Somehow, she knew, because she squeezed me until I couldn't breathe. Kovo parked their car and walked over. Rather than start babbling, like she usually did, Adrian stared at me with an awkward look on her face. Kovo wouldn't look at me at all.

What the hell? "Okay. What's with the weird looks?" I looked from one to the other. "And why are you here?" Not that I wasn't thrilled to see them, but they usually called. It wasn't like Miami was next door and they were popping over to borrow an egg.

———

Velik

"You sure about this?" Helion himself sat across from me in the small shuttle. I didn't know he cared, but I appreciated his effort.

"Yes. She has chosen a human male. He is worthy of her. I will not interfere." Henry would take care of her. I repeated the thought over and over, so my beast couldn't argue.

"So be it. Gods protect you, warlord."

We waited in silence as the shuttle moved over the planet's surface. Uninhabited by any kind of civilization, the planet was home to a variety of large predatory creatures. They had no detectable language, but they were twice my height and covered in thick, nearly impenetrable scales. They formed family units, worked in groups and were evolving at their own pace.

They weren't like us, but they lived their life. Clearly intelligent, they attacked anything and everything that touched down on the surface.

The Coalition left them alone.

The Hive, however, had discovered a creature capable of taking down a fully armored beast, and set up a base complete with a high level Integration Unit to oversee the transformation of the creatures as quickly as possible.

The first one sent into battle had wiped out an entire unit of Prillon warriors. And their ship. Tore through the hull with its claws, shredded an armored troop transport like it was paper.

And that had been one of the males. The females were bigger, stronger, and meaner. Especially when protecting their young.

I had a feeling my Stefani would appreciate their ferocity.

"We're here, commander." The pilot's voice came over the comm. "Dropping for deployment."

That meant me. I was loaded with weapons and explosives. No food. Didn't plan on living long enough to get hungry. Wreak havoc, destroy the Hive base, and die with honor.

Helion took one last look at me and sighed. "I fucking hate this. I'm sorry, Velik."

I couldn't help it, I laughed.

"Opening the drop door. Gods protect you, warlord." The pilot's words drew me to my feet.

Helion held out my armored helmet. I looked at it, then shook my head. The air was tolerable. I didn't need it. And I sure as fuck didn't want to talk to anyone once I jumped out of this shuttle.

I walked to the drop door and leaped without looking back. It wasn't me, but my beast who landed in a crouch. His pain was a living, breathing thing.

The shuttle glided away as quietly as it had come. Helion stood, his outline visible, until the craft flew out of sight.

Mate. The beast's one word was both protest and question.

We are not worthy.

For the first time in a very long while, he didn't argue. Memories shuffled through my mind in quick review. The beast cataloguing his failures. To break free of the serum. To recognize our female when she needed us. To protect her when she suffered, pregnant and alone. He reached the same conclusion.

We are not.

16

"What is this?"

I'd invited them in and we'd gone straight to the kitchen, mostly because I knew Kovo had a bigger appetite than a teenage boy.

I ran my fingertips over the delicate symbols and swirls on the outside of the metal box. About the size of a shoebox, the piece was obviously heirloom, high quality, and very old. It didn't look exactly like gold, but it didn't look like anything else, either. It was unique.

"That belonged to Velik's grandmother. He wanted the girls to have it." Kovo's explanation made my heart skip a beat.

"He what?"

"He wanted Alena and Terra to have his grandmother's cuffbox. They were very close when Velik was growing up. The piece has sentimental value as well as practical." Kovo sounded like a lawyer informing me of the terms of Velik's last will and testament.

"Why are you telling me this? Why doesn't he just give it to them himself?" I found the delicate clasp and released it. Slowly, I lifted the lid to see what the beautiful antique held.

Mating cuffs. His and hers. They rested on a black material that looked softer than silk. The detail carved into the cuffs matched that on the outside of the box. Lining the edges were a handful of small pockets, in each pocket a glittering crystal about the size of an almond. They didn't appear to be jewelry. The crystals were not attached to pendants or bracelets that I could see.

Did they slip into the mating cuffs?

I lifted one of the smaller cuffs, turning it this way, and that, to look for a place to attach one of the crystals, but found none. They were stunning works of art. "These were his grandmother's?"

I glanced up from the female mating cuff to find Adrian wiping a tear from her eye. "Yes. They have been in his family for generations."

"What's wrong? Why are you crying?"

I looked at Kovo for answers, but his arms were crossed and he remained mute.

"Adrian?"

"Stefani?" She mocked me.

I glared. "Don't do that. Whatever you have to say, just say it."

She sighed and Kovo reached over to gently rub her back. She leaned into him, and I bit back tears of my own. Every second I missed Velik more.

Adrian took a deep breath. "I love you, and you know I will support you, no matter what."

"I know." We were twins. Even more important, we were

sisters who had survived growing up in a poor neighborhood with a single mother. Loyal didn't begin to describe our relationship.

"Henry is a great guy. And I know he spent a lot of time with you, helping you with the girls."

"What does any of this have to do with Henry?"

Adrian reached across the table to grab my hand. "I don't know why you chose him, but it's your choice. Not mine."

"What choice?" Was she implying that I wanted to be with Henry?

Kovo finally decided to butt in. "Normally, in situations such as this, the assets remain under the control of the warlord's family on Atlan. But with the birth of his daughters, Velik wanted to ensure his wealth transferred to them."

"To the twins? Why is he giving mating cuffs to the twins?"

He inclined his head. I realized he had totally misunderstood my question as soon as he spoke. "A warlord's wealth is extensive, Stefani. You know this. Your father has accepted the role of guardian, at Velik's behest. He will maintain the properties and assets until such time as the girls come of age, or in the event you should relocate to Atlan." He cleared his throat. "I would have accepted the responsibility myself, but I can never return to Atlan. For this reason, the duty belongs to your father, the twins' grandfather."

"I don't understand. Why doesn't Velik just take care of it himself?"

"He cannot. He is not your mate. He has been deemed unworthy."

"By who?"

"By you, Stef. He told us you were going to be with Henry. That Henry asked you to marry him and then you let him hold you right in front of Velik's beast." Adrian said the words like they were part of a big scandal.

"I—technically. Yes. But I'm not going to marry Henry. He moved out. And he wasn't holding me. It was a hug. He was upset. I was upset. He's one of my best friends."

Kovo's scowl darkened with disapproval. "Atlans do not share their mates with other males."

"It wasn't sharing."

"Did you not also beg for this male's life, when Velik would have fought for you?" Kovo demanded.

"I didn't want Henry to get hurt. He's human. Velik's a beast. Velik could have killed him."

"You love him, your Henry?" Kovo asked.

"Yes. Of course, but not like that."

"There is no other way." As if that decided the matter, Kovo flipped the box around and reached inside to remove one of the small crystals. He held it up to the light and I noticed there appeared to be a series of fine lines and patterns buried deep within. They added to the sparkling effect when the sunlight struck. "These crystals contain encoded details and access keys to Velik's estate, his lands, everything he owns. Terra and Alena need only present these on our home world, and they will assume control of everything, under their grandfather's guidance and protection, of course."

"Where's Velik? You two aren't making any sense. I want him to explain this to me."

Adrian whispered. "He's gone."

"I know. He went back to Miami yesterday. But I just tried to call him. I sent him a text." I took the opportunity to check my phone. Nothing. "I'm just waiting for him to call back. I miss him."

"Oh, god." My sister looked like she was going to be sick, right there on the table. "You said Henry moved out?"

"Yeah, last night. When I told him I couldn't marry him."

"Why would you tell him that?" Adrian seemed shocked.

"Because I'm in love with a stupid Atlan, that's why."

The silence was thick with tension as I stared at my sister, then her mate, then back to my sister.

Kovo slipped the crystal back inside the box and gently closed the lid. "There will be no call, my sister."

"Why not? Did he forget who I am again? Because he was here less than twenty-four hours ago, kissing me. Where. Is. He? Just freaking tell me."

"He left. Last night."

"Left where?"

"The planet." Adrian wiped a fresh tear from her cheek and ice cold dread exploded inside me. "He's gone. Transported back out into space. He left to go on a mission."

"A suicide mission?" My voice was far calmer than I felt.

"There is no disgrace in choosing an honorable death over execution."

"Shut-up, Kovo." I held my hand up, palm toward his stupid face, when he started to say more. The regret in Adrian's eyes was all the proof I needed.

"You are going to get me to Miami, like now. I am going to transport to wherever he is and stop him."

"Why would you do such a thing?" Kovo asked. "You rejected his claim and found his beast unworthy. His death is a mercy."

All. Or. Nothing.

Carmen's words came back to haunt me.

I stood up as a scream of denial, of rage, erupted from my throat.

"I'm playing my twin card, every card I have. You owe

me, Adrian. You know you do." I looked her in the eye and willed her to remember the risks I'd taken to help her sneak into an Atlan prison cell and save Kovo. "I need you to stay here with the twins. I want a private jet, the fastest thing there is. And then I'm going to transport off this stupid planet and stop him from killing himself over a stupid hug I gave a man I'm not in love with!"

"There is more to your rejection of his claim than a mere hug." Kovo seemed unmoved by the rising panic in every cell of my body.

"He's mine. He's mine and he's not allowed to die." I pleaded with him, with my sister. "I was stupid. I get it. He hurt me and I didn't want to hurt like that again."

"Stef, he might be dead already."

"No!" This wasn't happening. "Private plane. I don't care about the coalition and their stupid rules. I'm going to Miami, I'm getting on that transport pad, and I'm going to stop him."

Kovo's lips moved.

"Shut up. I love my sister, but if you try to stop me, I'll kill you myself."

Adrian took my hand. "Are you sure?"

"Twin card. Playing it now. Why am I still here?" I looked at Kovo expectantly. "Let's go. You're driving."

I pulled, trying to break Adrian's grip, but she held tight, her fingers wrapped around me hard enough to hurt.

"I was hoping you would say that." Adrian turned my hand so my palm was face up and placed an alien disk of some kind in the center.

"What's that?"

"A transport beacon."

Kovo startled. "Where did you get that? Only the I.C. has access, and they don't like to share."

Adrian's eyes focused on mine. I stared back into the mirror image of my own face. "I got it from Warden Egara. After Velik left."

She paused to let me process what she was saying. Transport beacon. I didn't need to go to Miami to get off this planet. Bless that woman.

"She thought you might want to go after him. It's already programmed to his last known coordinates, to wherever the warden sent him. All you have to do is put it on and activate the signal."

"Oh my god, I love you."

"I love you, too." Our hug could have cracked ribs. "Go. I've got your girls. Go get him."

I pressed the transport beacon to my blouse and looked down. Polyester blouse. Cotton capri pants. Slip on sandals. Not exactly space battle attire.

Who fucking cared? I'd been a complete idiot. Velik needed me. They had clothes there.

I grabbed the box from the table, tucked it under my arm and held Adrian's gaze as I activated the beacon.

———

Velik

I DRAGGED the Hive Soldier's body to the edge of the ravine and pushed him over. No need to scan this one, as I normally would. This Hive was a creature not from the Coalition Fleet. There was no known family to notify of his death.

And the creature was male. The scattered remains of more than twenty more just like him littered the ground below. So far, I had not encountered a single female the Hive had managed to integrate.

Perhaps the females were even more dangerous than I believed. And more difficult for the Hive to control.

As if any creature on any planet could truly control their females.

My beast huffed in agreement as we watched a group of hungry creatures surround my newest kill. They were hungry, and not above scavenging for a meal. Feeding them the blood and bones of my enemies kept them away from my hunting grounds.

Like a shadow at the top of the cliff, I watched the carnage. The sounds of tearing flesh made my beast want to howl in satisfaction.

I lifted my face to this world's oddly colored, green star, and closed my eyes. I swayed on my feet. Blood flowed freely from multiple wounds on my body. Even Coalition armor could not withstand the creature's claws. Hunger clawed through my gut. I ignored it. I had no rations with me, only water. The plants here were toxic, not fit to eat. Not that it mattered.

I'd lost track of the hours I'd been hunting. Killing. My mission was not complete. No matter how many newly created Scouts and Soldiers I eliminated, I would not be finished until I destroyed the Integration Units.

They hid underground and sent these creatures out to fight me in their stead. Cowards.

I wondered how many foot soldiers they had left protecting them. According to the mission brief, our ReCon units had counted no more than thirty. Which meant at least ten remained? Perhaps more?

This planet could not become the newest Hive conquest. Battleship Zeus guarded the system. They'd spent long weeks driving the Hive from this sector of space. The final threat was here. On the ground.

I would end it. Protect the fleet. The Coalition of Planets.

Protect *her*.

Mate.

I hadn't argued. She was our mate, the female we had chosen. If we could not serve at her side, we would destroy her enemies. Keep her safe the only way left to us.

Once I eliminated the Hive Integration Units responsible for the newest Hive puppets, I would seek out one of the female creatures and test her.

No doubt, she would kill me.

In the distance, another Hive creature roared in challenge. The sound they made completely different from the bellows of their wild kin. This one was driven by the need to hunt and kill, not survive.

My beast responded in kind.

17

*S*tefani, Battleship Zeus, Intelligence Core, Restricted Transport Room

EVERY BONE in my body ached. My knees gave out at the sudden need to support my weight. I stumbled onto my hands and knees, palms pressed flat on the smooth, hard surface I recognized as a transport pad. The energy around me was thick as soup in the air, humming through me and making my hair want to stand on end.

Every time I moved, my polyester shirt crackled with static electricity. Yep. This transporting thing was just as much fun as I remembered.

"Don't move!" The harsh order was immediately followed by the stomping of more than one pair of boots.

"No problem." I was going to need a minute. I didn't know where I was, or how far I had zip-zapped through outer space, but something told me this place was far, *far* away from home.

God, that hurt! I'd forgotten exactly how much. It had

been a while since Adrian and I visited our mother on Atlan. Our mother promised us then we'd get used to it.

I still didn't believe her.

"How did you acquire the transport coordinates to this pad?" The business end of a space gun slipped under my bowed head. The Coalition fighter holding the weapon decided to use the hard tip to lift my chin.

Rather than argue or try to explain myself, I removed the transport beacon from my blouse and tossed it at his feet.

I'd only seen a handful of Prillon warriors. This one looked startled and genuinely at a loss. His tone, when he spoke to me again, was not *quite* as hostile. "Where did you get this, my lady?"

"Warden Egara." The new voice who answered the question was older. Calmer.

"Sir?"

Ah, so this was the guy in charge. Good.

The new arrival, yet another Prillon—did any of these aliens come in less than extra-extra-large?—walked to my side and helped me stand. Took me a minute of staring, but his face was one I would never forget. He'd been there, with Velik, the day I'd lost him. The day he'd nearly died and then forgotten who I was.

And he was wearing green. A doctor. *The doctor.*

"You're Helion."

He dipped his chin. "And you are Stefani Davis."

"I am." I tried a half-hearted smile at the guard who'd been threatening to floss my teeth with his rifle. Nope. Wasn't feeling it. "Where am I?"

"In Coalition controlled space, Sector 438. We are in orbit around a pale blue star labeled 438-5-18-42."

"Never mind. It doesn't matter." None of that made any sense to me after the word 'space'.

"You, my lady, have arrived in a secure transport facility aboard Battleship Zeus known only to the commander himself and members of the Intelligence Core who serve directly under my command."

"Top secret, huh?" No wonder the first Prillon had been so aggressive. I'd just landed in the middle of a super-secret military zone.

"Exactly."

"You don't seem surprised to see me."

"Catherine told me you might be coming."

"Catherine?"

"Apologies. Warden Egara." He nudged me forward and I took a few tentative steps. The movement helped. My body started working again. "I have known her many years. She was mate to my brother."

"Her mates died."

"Yes, they did."

Oh, shit. I was being an insensitive jerk. Not purposely, I just couldn't get my brain to work. "I'm sorry. Your brother..."

"It was a long time ago."

I thought about Warden Egara and shook my head. Not long enough for her to forget. She'd lost her mates. I was here to make sure I didn't lose mine.

"Where is he?"

Helion didn't even try to pretend he didn't know exactly who I was talking about. "He is on the surface of the fourth planet, hunting."

"When is he coming back?"

"He is not."

"That's what I thought." I shoved the Prillon away, not

wanting to touch the asshole who had sent my mate to die. "I'm going down there."

"That is not wise, my lady."

"Then go get him."

"That is impossible."

"Why?"

"Warlord Velik refused to wear a helmet. He deactivated both his imbedded transport beacon and his comm a few minutes after his landing." Before I could ask, Helion told me. "He cut them from his flesh. He does not wish to be found."

"I don't care what he thinks he wants. He's not dying down there. Do you understand? He's mine. And I'm going to go get him."

"You intend to go to the planet's surface?"

"I don't intend, I'm going."

He inspected the box I held. "Mating cuffs?"

"Don't leave home without 'em."

Helion actually smiled. "Depending on Velik's state of mind when we find him, you are going to need them." His smile faded and I saw a debate rage behind his eyes.

"What?"

"The planet is hostile. Extremely dangerous. You could be killed. I cannot guarantee your safety."

"Don't try to scare me. Just give me something to wear." I looked at the array of weaponry chosen by the large warriors in the room. "And one of those space guns." I looked up to find Helion watching me. "Don't worry, I know how to shoot."

"You, Stefani Davis, are very much like your sister."

"She's the nice one."

He chuckled and turned away from me to speak to the handful of fighters in the room. There weren't many, but if they worked with Helion, they were basically the Coalition's equivalent to our Navy SEALS, except in outer space. *Space SEALS* just didn't sound right.

I didn't care what they were called. I knew who and what they were. These were the guys who got shit done.

"You heard the lady. Suit up."

elik

The ReCon team had missed a few minor details.

There were over fifty of these fuckers already integrated —not thirty—and three of them were female. I had yet to fight one of the much larger females. I was not looking forward to the experience.

As all Hive did, these creatures hunted and fought in packs of three. Always groups of three, and they were ugly as fuck. Protruding scale heads with multiple sets of eyes, they could see in all directions at once, making it impossible to sneak up on them. Their stance reminded me of Earth's orangutans, with crouching back legs and abnormally long arms and one massive claw protruding from the arm where a hand should be. The claws were sharp as fuck. Unlike Earth's great apes, these things were not cute or furry. The females were twice the beast's size and covered from head to toe in thick scales that were harder to pierce than Coalition armor.

The three massive female creatures stood guard outside

the underground base. The place I had come to this planet to destroy. They were the last of the Hive's work still alive and functioning on the planet's surface. Fifty-one of the integrated males now rested at the bottom of the ravine. Or what was left of them.

These things weren't the only predators on the planet.

ReCon had missed that bit of information as well. Although I didn't blame them. The second tier predators here were about half the size of those the Hive were integrating, much more animal with less intelligence, and slipped through the shadows at night without making a sound.

The Fleet would know now. My armor recorded everything that had occurred since my arrival, along with a few notes I added manually. In particular, tips on fighting the integrated creatures in hand-to-hand combat. They were fast as fuck when moving laterally. Forward or backward? They moved like sludge. That was *with* the Hive integration's assistance.

Without it? I had no idea. Perhaps my idea of forward and backward was incorrect, at least to them. If a creature had more than one set of eyes in its head, which direction was the front?

Stupid. Don't care.

The beast was tired. So was I. And the large female creatures hadn't responded to any of my efforts to pull them away from their job guarding the entrance. I'd caught one of their males and tortured him until his screams nearly made me deaf.

The females had tilted their heads to listen, but not taken a single step in my direction to save him.

Males not worthy.

Of course. Like us. The females did not need these

particular males for mating. They were unimportant. Not worth the risk.

Not worthy.

"Stop talking, beast." Fuck. I didn't need to hear those two words again. Ever. My beast had been repeating them at every opportunity since the moment we'd left Stefani behind.

We had done the honorable thing. The right thing for her, and for our daughters. A male of worth never forced his attention on his chosen female. We had to be invited in and accepted in return. Deemed worthy to touch, to claim, to father children. A male must be chosen. A female mate must agree to the final claiming, or it just didn't happen. The beast, as savage as he might be, was the last line of defense for his mate. Even from himself.

Our female wanted that blond human, Henry, to be her mate. So be it. We honored her choice. We made the sacrifice to ensure her happiness. Still fucking hurt like she'd ripped our heart out and thrown it down that ravine for the scavengers to devour.

Fuck Henry.

I agreed with my beast, but the decision wasn't ours. It was hers. Our mate.

Mate. Mine! Not worthy. The beast howled in despair inside my mind. I couldn't stop him. He was going to drive me over the edge. Not acceptable. I kept reminding him we couldn't die until the mission was complete. We had to defeat the three female creatures, kill the Hive Integration Unit—their version of a doctor—and destroy their base of operations so they would never attempt to integrate these creatures again. Protecting the Coalition Fleet and all the fighters meant protecting *her*.

Then we could end our misery.

"Almost, my friend. Almost." Was I trying to reassure the beast, or myself?

I held a ReCon team's newest scanner to my eyes and reviewed the data as it scrolled across the small, built-in screen. Distance to the base. Size and estimated weight of each female, as well as the type of weapon they carried.

Not that the creatures needed any help. They already had hides thicker than battle armor and those fucking claws. Maybe the Hive armed them with technology out of habit.

The males I'd taken out had come at me claws first, as if their ion blasters were a mere afterthought.

Maybe. Or maybe they just enjoyed ripping and tearing flesh.

My beast snorted, clearly suspecting the latter.

Sliding down, so I would be out-of-sight on the ridge, as well as downwind of the creatures, I took final stock of my gear.

Power cells on the ion rifle were shot. As were the two spares I'd brought with me. In fact, I'd used up everything I had but the blades strapped to my thighs and a handful of small explosive devices. I'd planned on using them to destroy the base, but that wouldn't be possible if I couldn't get inside to set the charges.

I had to get past those guards.

Death trap.

The beast wasn't afraid of death, or the creatures, but he wasn't stupid either. If we charged over the ridge and tried to fight them, we would lose. Head cut from our body and eaten for an afternoon snack, kind of lose.

I wondered what my daughters were doing today. Eating the smashed bananas they loved? Playing with their soft toys? Napping? My heart ached as I pictured their beautiful, adoring smiles the last and final time I sang to them.

Not worthy.

"Shut the fuck up. I know." Did Henry sing to them?

Did Stefani sing? How could I not know this about her?

You left. Let them kill me.

"I didn't fucking let them do anything. I was unconscious."

Weak. Not worthy.

"FUCK!" No wonder warlords who were not accepted by their mates didn't live long. And not just because of mating fever. But because, "Their fucking beast won't shut up."

I looked at the explosives.

I'd just have to blow the female creatures into pieces and figure out how to destroy the base after. If I had to sit here and listen to the beast's whining for another minute, I was going to lose my mind.

Weak, Not—

"Fuck you." It was stupid, I knew it, but it was time. I hit the transmit button on my armor. My entire battle log and all the data I'd collected about the life forms on this planet would be uploaded to the Coalition Fleet's system before I was halfway to the three females.

Seemed fitting a fucking female would kill me, as I'd treated one of their own so poorly.

I forced my body into rhythm. Running. Planning as I went. When the first creature was in sight, I sprinted toward her. She swung her long arms, her reach the length of my entire body when one included the claws—at me with the intention of cutting me in half.

They were bigger than their males, but they were also slower. And they fought exactly the same way.

I'd just killed fifty-one of her closest friends. I knew how they moved.

If I'd been trying to kill her outright, I'd have lost before I'd begun. But I didn't need to kill her. I just needed to slap the explosive to her body, somewhere in the middle, and move out of reach before she sliced through my body like a blade through water.

I slipped under her slashing claws and spun, slamming the explosive on her back as I went. Staying directly behind her—or at least in the direction I knew they lumbered slowly, I ran out of its reach and straight at the second female.

The first bellowed in rage and turned to follow me. When she moved, the second answered.

I'd been counting on this as well. Each of these creatures seemed eager to kill, and willing to fight their own kind for the chance to do so.

Vicious fucking things. No wonder the Hive wanted to utilize them so badly.

The bomb-laden creature stopped, waiting to destroy me if this one failed. I repeated my movements almost exactly. Duck the swinging claws, run beneath them. Get behind the creature. Slap on the second explosive. Run!

Right onto the claw of number three.

Too fucking smart.

She must have watched me with the first two and antici-pated my movements. Sloppy. I should have anticipated this. But I was too tired. I looked down at the tip of the claw embedded in my gut and I felt nothing. No pain. No fear. The clarity in that moment was a surprise, but then, I'd never watched myself die before.

Methodically, purposely, I removed the last two explo-sives from my armor. One I tossed toward the opening of the base. It wouldn't destroy the base completely, but it should do enough damage to trap the Integration Unit inside. With the creatures all dead, it would be easy for a ReCon team to finish the job.

The last explosive I held in my right hand. With my left, I pulled the blade from its holster on my thigh and waited.

I'd seen this ending before as well. Piercing strike to their prey. Inspection. Once the prey item was deemed edible, the creature would raise its second claw and slice me in half. The bottom half would fall to the ground and be pierced by that second claw literally the second it hit the ground. They used their claws like eating utensils.

This time, I was lunch. But she was going to swallow a bomb. All I had to do was wait for the slight movement of that second claw to activate it.

Dangling in mid-air, I stared into the creature's eyes, all six of them on this side of her skull and waited. Too long. She should have sliced me in half by now.

Pain. Sharp, agonizing pain roared through me. Pain from so many injuries I'd lost count. From her claw. The hundreds of small bruises and cuts on my body. The despair of losing Stefani.

We stared at one another, two monsters, neither moving. The liquid silver in her eyes was not her own. It was Hive. I knew exactly who was watching me, not this poor wild thing, but the true monster hiding inside the base, using these creatures as his puppets.

"I'm sorry." I spoke to the female creature I was about to burn alive from the inside out, not the Hive mind inside her.

An explosion sounded behind me. Gore rained down from above, the goopy leftovers from the first monster's carcass. The second exploded. The shockwave strong enough to shove my body farther onto the creature's claw.

Her free arm lifted.

I set the timer on the incendiary device for two minutes. I wanted to be deep in her gut when it detonated. There would be nothing but ash left, of either of us.

Her claw swung toward my hips.

I thought of Stefani. Her scent. Her skin. Her screaming 'no' like I imagined she did when I abandoned her. When I failed her.

Her voice. It sounded so real.

The explosive I'd thrown a few moments ago exploded at the base's entrance. The creature holding me stumbled sideways from the shock of the blast. She lowered her free claw to steady her large frame. Stood once more. Lifted that same claw to finish what she'd started.

Her head exploded right in front of me. The creature went rigid. Dust from the rock around the base's entrance rained down in a fine powder, coating me in a layer of dust that stuck to the gore already covering me from head to foot.

She fell and I fell with her, landing on my left side, still impaled on her claw.

I looked to my right to confirm I still held the last weapon. Fire. An inferno. I had to see the disk because I could feel...nothing.

It was there. I wrapped my hand around the device as tightly as I could manage.

Good. We would both burn.

———

*S*TEFANI

. . .

WHAT *WAS* THAT *THING*? It was twice Velik's size, but its arms hung down its sides like an orangutang's. It wasn't just an arm. There were claws on the ends of them that looked like they were longer than my arms. Instead of fur, they were covered in heavy scales that looked like a cross between an alligator and a sea turtle. The mouth and teeth? T-Rex. The top of its head was disgusting. Too many eyes, on more than one side. They were creepy, set in groups, like a spider's.

One of them had stabbed Velik and looked like it was about to eat him.

"Helion! Do something!" I was frantic. Velik moved, thank god. He'd dodged the first two—I'd thought I was having a heart attack—but there were *three* of those things. Three.

"Working on it." I chanced taking my eyes off my mate to see Helion and another one of the Prillon warriors who accompanied us, each settled on one knee, a tripod looking thing in front of each of them. On top of the tripods? Two really big space guns. Thank god.

"Shoot it."

"We will."

"Now!"

Another Prillon warrior, who stood on my opposite side, placed a gentle hand on my shoulder. "My lady, they must not miss."

No shit.

"There are three of them. They're going to kill him."

"Have faith. Your mate placed explosive devices on the first two. This battle is not yet lost."

Explosives? I examined the creature on the far right, the one Velik had charged first. I didn't see anything except a black disk attached to the creature's side. The disk was about the size of my hand. Was that what the Prillon was talking about? It looked like a gnat compared to that monster. I searched the second monster's body, looking for the same thing. Couldn't find one, but maybe it was on the other side, facing away from me. That first disk was so small, if the Prillon hadn't told me it was there, I never would have noticed.

Then again, a little thing the size of a coin had transported me halfway across the galaxy—or all the way. I still had no idea where the hell I was in relation to Earth. Didn't care. When it came to alien stuff, small didn't mean it wasn't powerful.

I hoped it was a million times stronger than C-4.

Velik. I whimpered. I couldn't stop the sound. One of the creatures had stabbed all the way through him with one claw, the tip visible, protruding from Velik's back. His legs were swinging in the air, not because he was trying to get away, but because he *wasn't* fighting. He was limp.

I wrapped my arms around my stomach, the pain visceral. He had to be hurting. So much. So, so much. Tears ran unchecked down my face.

How was he still alive?

A loud booming sound made me jump. The first monster exploded like a paint ball, guts and gore splattered everywhere. It even rose high in the air and came back down to splatter everything in the immediate area. Including Velik.

I gagged. God. Velik. This was a nightmare. No, worse than that. This was true horror. If this was what the warlords in the Coalition Fleet had to deal with, they deserved more than an Interstellar Bride. More than a few castles, or lands, or tons of cash.

Nothing would ever be enough. There was *nothing* that could make up for *this.*

The second explosion wasn't as much of a shock. The placement on the monster must have been different, because this one's parts didn't spread quite as far as the first. Half of its body was still in one piece, or mostly one piece, on the ground.

The third explosion made me jump even though I was expecting it this time. It didn't destroy the last monster. It blew up what was obviously a door of some kind. The rocks and dirt from the ridge above it collapsed, tumbling down the side of the hill like rolling thunder, an avalanche of debris. The rubble blocked the entrance, but left the last creature unscathed.

The force of the blast *did* knock over the one holding my mate on its claw like a shish-kabob.

The monster caught itself, using one of those long claws like a hand to brace its weight against the ground. The thing regained its balance. Lifted its free claw. Swung it toward Velik.

"No!" My scream was instinctive. I had to get to my mate.

The Prillon next to me, the one whose hand I'd forgotten remained on my shoulder, pulled me back when I bolted forward, uncaring of the danger. I had to get to Velik.

"Let me go!"

The Prillon warrior shook his head and tightened his grip. "It is not safe."

"I don't care."

"He does." The warrior pointed in Velik's direction.

I swung on Helion, ready to shove him out of the way and fire his weapon myself.

No need. High pitched buzzing made me flinch as two blasts of light exited the nozzles.

Almost instantly, the monster's head exploded into bloody mist. Poof. Gone. Vaporized.

The thing was dead, but my mate was still hanging in the air, a claw through his body.

Helion gave an order to approach. The Prillon holding me looked me in the eye and ordered me to stay next to him. I said nothing.

I'd stay next to him as long as he was going where I wanted to go.

To Velik.

I didn't take my eyes off my mate as I moved forward with the group. Helion took point, which seemed odd, for a doctor, but what did I know about military operations. Nothing.

We were close to the first monster. The stench of the dead creatures made my eyes water and my throat burn. Pungent, like cigar smoke and burning hair with a side-order of melting plastic.

Was that smell coming from their guts? Or their scaly body armor?

I looked at the headless creature still holding Velik. Standing there like nothing had happened, even without its head. The thing's body remained upright.

Until. God! The monster's entire body fell to one side like a tree falling over. It hit the ground and didn't move. So did Velik, the huge claw still embedded in his body from front to back, like a sword.

Velik didn't move.

No. No. No.

I started running. To him. My mate. My Velik.

"Velik!" I screamed his name as I closed the distance. I was shocked when he managed to turn his head in my direction. His gaze was cloudy, unfocused. The closer I got, the clearer his eyes became.

"No! Stay back!" His voice was a command, pure and

simple. I'd never heard that tone, not from any of the Atlans I knew. He meant it. Down to his soul, meant it. He didn't want me anywhere near him.

I stumbled and fell to my knees. I deserved his hatred. I so did. Sobbing, I crawled toward him, begging. "Please, Velik. I'm so sorry." I reached a hand toward him.

"No! Fuck!" He twisted, his cry of pain piercing as the claw cut more of his insides. He tossed something away from him. With a loud roar, his beast came out, the shift in his size faster than any I'd seen. The beast bellowed with pain.

"No! Velik! Don't move! There's a ReGen pod. Don't move!"

The beast ignored me, just like Velik had.

"Stay back!"

I stopped crawling toward him, unsure what to do. The others, Helion and the Prillon warriors, were busy shooting at...something. Whatever it was, it was moving quickly, running along the top of the avalanche area, shooting back.

I didn't even look up to try to figure out who or what was there. I didn't care. There was only one reason I was here.

"Velik." Holding myself back, I lifted one hand from the ground and reached for him. "Please. I'm so sorry. Let me help you!"

"No!" He drove one elbow into the hard ground. Pulled.

The sound of the blade tearing his flesh, sucking at the wound, made me scream. "Stop it! Don't move!"

"Worthy."

What?

Another elbow. Another pull. More blood soaked the ground. I shook my head, tears streaming down my face. Why? Why was he doing this?

He pulled to his side. He groaned as I watched him cut

himself open. He moved to his side. I watched in shock as the piece of claw protruding from his back slid—cut—through his body, moving in a slow, steady line from the puncture site to the edge of his armor. Then beyond. Velik rolled free, his self-inflicted wound easily the length of my hand, wrist to fingertip.

Shit! What was he doing?

He lunged to his knees. Then his feet. He stumbled toward me.

I tried to get up. To reach for him.

"No!" He drew in a deep, rattling breathe that I knew meant his lungs were filling with blood. "Cover!"

He screamed the warning and threw his body on top of mine, curling himself around me.

Something exploded, the sound like lightning striking the ground right next to us.

Fire roared above our heads as if someone was shooting a flamethrower at us.

It blasted past, then receded as quickly as it had come. My ears were ringing, but I wasn't hurt. Velik's battered body had taken most of the blast.

Wrapped around me, he didn't move. I didn't dare. The heat of his body mixed with the warmth of his blood. The only way I knew the difference was when a soaked area of the lightweight armor Helion had given me clung to my skin. Wet.

"Velik."

"Mate."

His beast whispered the word but disappeared right after as Velik transformed back into his normal self. By choice? Or because he was too weak to hold the form of his beast? I didn't know.

Every breath he took rattled in his chest. The horrible

wound in his torso had collapsed in on itself, so it was difficult to see any detail around his black armor. The injury was
there. The blood was proof of that. And what I could see?
His striking face and strong jaw? The lips that had kissed
me, that I had kissed? Every single part of his head and neck
was covered in dust-clotted *gore*.

He was beautiful. So strong. So gentle and protective
and perfect.

And very much mine.

Even if I had to bring his beast back from the dead all
over again, this beast was mine.

I lifted a hand and wiped the heavy gunk away from his
eyes. His cheeks. His mouth. I cleared what I could. He was
conscious, I knew by the arm he wrapped around me,
holding me close.

I looked around his large body as much as I could. No
one was here. I remembered them running and shooting at
something on the ridge. Most of the team was gone, probably chasing the enemy—or whoever had been firing on
them—to a place beyond where I could see them. Only one
Prillon remained within shouting distance, the one who'd
put his hand on my shoulder, been my shadow since we got
on the shuttle to come down here. He must have remained
behind as my guard.

I couldn't drag Velik back to our shuttle, he was too
heavy and it was too far. I wouldn't dare, even if I could,
afraid I would do the one wrong thing that would kill him.

I wrapped my arms around Velik's head and held him as
close as I could, cradled his cheek to my chest and hoped he
would be comforted by the sound of my thundering heart. It
was beating for him.

I held him. I loved him. I screamed for help.

19

*S*tefani, Battleship Zeus, Eight Days Later

I REFUSED to leave his side. Not this time. If Helion or that other one, Mersan, walked toward Velik's ReGen pod with *anything* in their hands, I demanded a full explanation before I let them near my mate. Details. What was it called? What was it for? Why did Velik need it?

No more experimental serum to kill Velik's beast. No poison to erase his memory. He was nearly healed. I considered it a miracle he'd lived long enough to get back to the ship. I wasn't taking a chance now.

Leaning over, I rested my forehead against the translucent cover and watched him sleep—or whatever someone did when they were in these things. Hibernate? Was it like a coma? I had no idea.

"Wake up. Velik. I'm here. I'm never leaving you again. Please wake up."

The doctors and other medical people—they didn't call

them nurses so I wasn't sure about the official title—had, to a man, promised me Velik was going to make a full recovery.

Guess I had Helion to thank for Velik's life. Helion, my sister, and Warden Egara. The women, especially, had figured out what I was going to do before I did it. They'd seen through the lies I'd been telling myself before I did.

Wasn't that always the way it worked? Especially if you had a sister who knew you almost as well as she knew herself? Maybe better?

I couldn't stop seeing Velik drag his body on the ground to get to me. Force that monster's claw to cut him all the way through to his side. What he'd done was unbelievable. And all to protect me. To be worthy of being loved.

The thought made me want to cry. He was more than worthy. In fact, I didn't deserve him. I knew it. I'd been selfish and obsessed with protecting myself. I didn't deserve him. *I* wasn't worthy. I didn't fucking care. I was keeping him anyway.

I lifted my arm so I could use my forearm as a pillow and watched him sleep inside the pod.

After Helion and his team finished hunting what I'd later learned was a special kind of Hive alien that did Integrations—which Helion explained was adding all the creepy technology that took control of a fighter's mind and body—Helion worked some paramedic, battlefield style, emergency medicine on Velik before the others carried him back to the shuttle.

Helion had tried to treat me, once the shuttle was on the way back to the battleship. I smacked his hand away and ordered him to take care of my mate. He chuckled, but I meant it. Velik was a mess with a capital M.

And now, he wasn't.

He just needed to wake up—and forgive me for putting

mating cuffs on his wrists when he was out cold. I had mine on as well. The doctor had offered to adjust them—as they had recently for human brides—so they would not cause me pain if I were to be more than—I wasn't sure of the exact distance. I didn't care. If I could take care of my own—baby wipe—business, alone, in the bathroom without the things hurting me, I was good.

I refused the doctor's offer. I didn't want to be separated from Velik. Never again.

"He's going to be angry when he learns you have not been caring for yourself properly." Doctor Mersan, who'd I'd started to think of as *Coppertop,* because of his copper colored hair and dark, nearly black eyes, said something annoying every time I saw him. I was beginning to think Helion was the sweet one.

"I'm fine."

"You removed the bloodied armor, true. But you have not cleansed your body properly."

"I used baby wipes." I'd ordered them from the S-Gen machine and wiped myself down, discreetly, when I knew I'd have a few minutes between medical people walking in.

"Baby wipes?"

Did I want to tell this arrogant alien what baby wipes were *normally* used for? It was a good thing I had my head down. I was quite certain my smile was downright evil.

"It's not important. I wiped myself off. I used the S-Gen to get some comfy clothes." A pair of yoga pants, a hoodie, and a pair of slip on shoes lined with fluff so my toes wouldn't get cold. "And I ordered food from the S-Gen, too. I'm fine."

I stared at my mate through the glass. He was like Snow White under there. Velik was so handsome. I looked him over, especially the terrifying wound from that giant claw.

There was nothing there but a very thin line. If I wasn't looking for it, I wouldn't have been able to see it.

His eyelids twitched. I waited for more, hoping he was waking up. But no. I sighed.

"Ms. Davis."

"I have a mate." I had the mating cuffs on my wrists to prove it and I wasn't taking them off.

He sighed. "My lady, I reviewed the records of the S-Gen machine you have been utilizing. There have been only three orders for food over the last four days. You cannot nourish your body properly on liquids alone."

"I'm fine, Doc. I promise. I don't need much." Besides, my stomach was so upset, my nerves raw, my worry over Velik spending so long in the ReGen pod. When I closed my eyes all I saw was those monsters trying to kill him. I was so on edge, so frazzled, that I couldn't keep much down anyway. Even the *thought* of most foods made me nauseous. It was even worse than when I was pregnant...

Oh shit. No.

I did some lighting fast mental math. Eight days in ReGen pod, plus one day after he left California, three more days he spent with the girls, and the day before that?

Hot sex. Hot, begging, shove me against the wall, sex. If I'd gotten pregnant *that day?* I pressed my hand over my tummy and held it there. Was there new life growing inside me right *now?* Was I really *that fertile?*

Two weeks from conception to puking? Oh yes. Just like last time. Totally possible. The math worked. I. Was. Pregnant.

More babies? The twins weren't even walking yet? What if I had twins again?

I would absolutely have twins. The knowledge was

there, rock solid. I was pregnant. Again. With twins. More girls. Four little girls.

Four babies *at the same time*? *Four* little ones to take care of, all under the age of two?

I couldn't breathe. I doubled over and braced myself against the pod. In. Out. Air. It was easy. Deep breath in through the nose. Out through the mouth.

Again.

"My lady? What is it? What is wrong?" The doctor approached me with one of those fancy scanners. I bolted to the opposite side of the ReGen pod. If I *was* pregnant, I didn't want the official news from a coppertop alien while the father was laying here unconscious.

The seal of the ReGen pod broke with a quiet hiss. The translucent cover retracted into the base. Velik sat up, said nothing and pulled me onto his lap. He looked over his shoulder at the doctor and ordered the guy to leave. Which Mersan did, without a word.

"Mate, why do you smell of those creatures?"

"I—"

He leaned in close, his nose in the curve of my neck. "I heard the words spoken. You have not eaten? Nor bathed? You have refused to take care of yourself? Why are you doing this? Do you seek to punish me?"

"What? No!" I wrapped my arms around him and leaned in. "I was afraid to leave. Last time you were in a ReGen pod—"

He spoke softly, his lips moving over the skin on my neck. "Shhh. We will not speak of it."

"Okay."

"You agree?" He lifted his head and there he was, my mate, alive and well and close enough to kiss.

Suddenly I wished I'd showered, and brushed my teeth

at least once in the last twelve hours. "Can we get out of here?"

"Of course." Velik swung his legs over the side of the ReGen pod. He stood, cradling me to his chest, and walked out of the medical bay.

Naked. Bare assed, cock swinging in the wind, naked.

He carried me that way through what felt like the entire ship. We got a few looks. One female—looked like she was Prillon—opened her mouth to say something.

Velik growled at her.

She glanced down at...his cock, looked at me, laughed and moved out of the way. Once we were safely past her in the corridor, she called out to me. "Have fun!"

Velik carried me through some kind of cafeteria, causing a few eating utensils to freeze in midair, down another long corridor, into an elevator of some kind. By the time he carried me into what looked like a large hotel suite—bed, sofa, few basic items of furniture—I had no idea what was up, down, or sideways. And I was sure everyone on the ship had seen his magnificent backside. And frontside. All sides.

He carried me straight into the bathroom and stripped me of my clothing with an almost medical precision. Fuzzy slipper-socks. Yoga pants. He pulled the hoodie up over my head. I held out my hands so he could pull my arms free of the sleeves.

He froze. He didn't move, or speak. Did nothing but stare at the mating cuffs I'd put on my wrists.

And his. Had he not noticed them on his wrists before now?

"I'm sorry if—I shouldn't have put them on without asking. I hope you're not mad."

He stared. His face was smooth as granite. I had no idea what he was thinking

"I can take them off if—"

"No!" I thought the beast was about to come out of him. Instead, it was Velik who pulled my wrists together, held my hands in his, and knelt before me. "My lady, I have made many mistakes. I have caused you pain. I abandoned you when you needed me most. I know these things can never be forgiven." He dropped his forehead and lifted the back of my hands to his lips. "I am not worthy, Stefani. But I love you. You are mine. My mate. My brave, intelligent, strong female. You are beautiful. Perfect. I cannot let you go."

Everything he had suffered and survived. His devotion. The gifts of Terra and Alena, two daughters to love. His willingness to die so I could be with a human man he believed I loved.

This beast, this honorable man, knelt before me and believed *he* was not worthy of being loved?

"I have never known of anyone, warlord or warrior, more worthy than you. I love you." With gentle fingertips, I lifted his chin so I could look him in the eyes, so he would understand how deeply I loved him. "I claim you as my mate, Warlord Velik. I claim you as father to our children. I claim you as my lover and my friend. You are honorable, fearless and kind. I want you, so much. I am *so* proud of you." I cupped the side of his face with my small hand. He leaned into the touch, his gaze locked with mine. "I don't deserve you. I know I don't. I was an idiot, trying not to love you so I wouldn't get hurt. I fell in love with you anyway. There will never be a day of my life when I am not madly in love with you and your growly beast. I'm keeping you. I want to keep you. Both of you."

"I am yours."

Three words. My heart exploded with love for this male, this beast.

We washed one another quickly, especially once I explained that I wanted to spend hours with him—in bed.

The beast, apparently, complained. Velik told him he'd already had two turns while Velik had none. I hadn't really thought about it that way, but I could see his point.

We laid on the soft sheets facing one another, pillows under our cheeks. We took our time. I touched him everywhere. The scar was there. Faint.

I kissed every bit of it, all the way around his body as tears streamed down my cheeks. He kissed my tears away, and then he kissed me everywhere. He spent extra time over my abdomen. "Our children were here."

"Yes."

"By the gods, you are so beautiful. So fucking beautiful." He moved lower, his mouth working my clit until I was a writhing, moaning mess. He teased me, taking me to the edge of release over and over as I begged him to fill me up. Take me. Claim me.

Moving up my body, he sucked and kissed my breasts, my thighs spread wide to accommodate his shoulders. Higher, to kiss me. Long, deep, hungry kisses I would never get enough of.

Sex with the beast was frantic. Wild. Frenzied and desperate.

This was something more. A reckoning. Atonement. Two souls marking each other, claiming one another. Forever.

My body was on fire. I was desperate. Needy. But it was the love making me ache. It was so strong, so violent and alive. A living, breathing thing inside me. Too big to restrain, even when it hurt my heart to feel it.

He covered me with his body. His cock thrust deep.

So hard. Long. Before I could adjust to his size he was

moving, pushing deep. Pulling out to the very edge. Plunging inside me again. Over and over.

I arched my back off the bed, wrapped my leg around his thigh. I lifted my hips. Closer. I needed to be closer. I needed him deeper.

He grabbed my hands and held them in place over my head. Weight on that elbow, he slipped his other hand under my bottom and gave me what I wanted.

He fucked me. Thrust forward.

He lifted my hips, rubbed my clit against his rock hard body. Every movement he made, hard or fast, rough or gentle, rolled along my clit as his cock went deep.

My orgasm didn't build, it exploded, every muscle in my body rigid in ecstasy as the inner walls of my pussy pulsed and spasmed. He fucked me through it, never stopping. The moment the first orgasm ended, the second began.

"Velik!"

"You're mine. You're fucking mine. Mine. Mate. Mine."

The words matched the rhythm of his cock as it pushed deep. Pulled out. He said them over and over, as if he couldn't believe them.

"I love you."

His body went rigid. His cock swelled. Pulsed. Hot seed pumped into my body as he claimed me. Made me his... forever.

Three little words and I'd wrecked him. There was power there. Pleasure.

I'd have to remember that.

When we could breathe, he looked down into my eyes.

His cock swelled deep inside me where we remained joined. He hadn't left my body and I didn't want him to. We were connected. One.

My pussy reacted, tightening on his length, pulsing with heat. My heart raced.

He stared at me, unblinking. Intense. His dark eyes filled with tears, as if being loved caused him pain. His voice, when he spoke, was a whisper.

"Say it again."

EPILOGUE

elik, Two Weeks Later

MY MATE, my everything, walked through the hall of my family home with a soft smile on her face. I'd never seen her like this before. A traditional Atlan gown drifted down over her soft curves. She'd chosen to wear a dark, rich burgundy, the color of my favorite Atlan wine.

Her skin glowed. The mating cuffs we both wore were special. My grandparents had a wonderful life together. A deep, loving bond. This had been their home.

Now it as hers. If she approved.

If not? There were a dozen other places, equally beautiful, that I would acquire for her. Anything she wanted, I would provide. Anything. I could do nothing less. Her tears crushed me. Her joy made my heart sing. Her happiness was mine.

Being obsessed with one's mate had consequences. A warlord's happiness never again belonged to him alone.

The beast scoffed at my stupidity. Of course we would take care of her in all ways.

Mate. Mine.

I got it. She's mine, too, you know?

Not tonight. The beast thrust imagines into my mind, memories of our mate with her back to the wall, arms locked over her head, screaming with pleasure as he fucked her.

All right, beast. She likes you, too.

Love. Loves me.

Yes.

We both settled, content at the thought. Our mate loved us. Both of us. She told us every day, multiple times. And especially when we had our mouth on her wet pussy, or our cock deep in—

"Velik? What about the girls? Will they be accepted here? They're half human. I know they aren't going to any kind school yet, but I want them to be happy here as well."

I walked to where she stood, staring out a floor to ceiling window that overlooked my grandmother's favorite flower garden. I had spent many happy years there as a boy. "They will be admired, mate. They are the daughters of a warlord returned from the war. Not many of us return. Those that do are rewarded with vast wealth and places of honor in the government or military sectors. Every father wants his daughter to mate a warlord. We are quite popular."

I wrapped my arms around her from behind and pulled her back to rest against my chest. She melted into my arms, as she always did. That acceptance a gift, the value of which she would never comprehend.

"I love this house. It's peaceful. The gardens are gorgeous. I want a fresh start for us, Velik. I don't want to think about the past. I want us to be focused on the future."

"And your mother lives in this city with Warlord Maxus. You would be able to visit her often. Our daughters would know both of their grandmothers." My own mother, several aunts, uncles, cousins and other family members were scattered around the continent as well. But this estate was special to me.

This was a house that had always been full of love. I could feel it in the stones and the light that shone in through the windows. I hoped Stefani would feel it as well.

"Terra and Alena will race down the hallways, laughing. They will play in the garden. They will be safe and loved here. They will be happy." I turned her around to face me and leaned down to kiss her. "You, my mate, will be loved here. You will be happy. I vow it."

"Okay."

That word always surprised me. Acceptance, agreement, trust. All wrapped up in one response from my female.

"And in the future, if we want more children, there is more than enough room."

"In the future?"

"Of course. I love you, Stefani. I love Terra and Alena. I am content. But if you wanted more children, I would say, okay."

My mate tossed her head back and laughed. "Okay? You'd say okay? That's my word."

"Okay." This was fun, playing with words. Teasing her. Every moment with her took me farther and farther away from war. Darkness. Despair. She had no idea what she meant to me. None.

With a look on her face I did not recognize, she took my hand and placed it over her abdomen. "The future is here, Velik."

"I don't understand." Did she want me to slide my hand

lower, lift her skirt and tease her pussy with my fingers until she came all over my hand? Because that would, indeed, be an excellent way to say hello to the house.

"How many bedrooms does this place have?" she asked.

"Twelve." Bedrooms? Future bedrooms. For future children.

She placed one hand on top of mine where it remained pressed to her abdomen. She stepped closer. "Velik, love, I'm pregnant."

"But—"

"Once, for us, is apparently all it takes."

"How—"

She interrupted me again. "I went to my doctor this morning. I didn't want to say anything until I knew for sure."

We had just transported to Atlan a few hours ago so I could show her the house.

"This morning? On Earth?"

"Yes. I had the initial ultrasound. There were two heart-beats. Twins. Again. And every instinct I have is telling me they're girls." She looked up into my face.

Two more children? Mine? No warlord could be as blessed as I.

"Well? Did you hear me? Is it okay?"

Emotion clogged my throat. I could not speak. This could not be real, this life I did not deserve. Stefani, my mate. Terra and Alena, my beautiful daughters. And *two more?* Girls to protect and love. Care for. Serve. "I will be honored to be their father, as I am with Terra and Alena. I am not worthy of such a gift."

She raised an eyebrow and looked at me. "You really mean that."

"Of course. It is a male's greatest honor to be so blessed. To love and protect his family. I love you, Stefani Davis of

Earth. I am yours. If you wish for twenty more children or none, I am content. What you desire, you shall have. What you need, I will provide. You are mine. Our children will never doubt they are loved. You do not yet understand what being mine means, mate, but you will."

"You just can't be real."

"Okay."

"That's not how you use that word."

"Okay."

She laughed, the sound filling the hall with echoes of love. Joy. All things she brought to my life. "You are more than worthy, Velik. I love you."

I kissed her lips, softly. With great care. She was a goddess. My mate. Those words, those three fucking words. Powerful. They were a knife in my heart and a balm for the pain all in one. She owned me. Body. Mind. Soul. I was hers.

"Say it again."

A SPECIAL THANK YOU TO MY READERS...

Want more? I've got *hidden* bonus content on my web site *exclusively* for those on my <u>mailing list.</u>

If you are already on my email list, you don't need to do a thing! Simply scroll to the bottom of my newsletter emails and click on the *super-secret* link.

Not a member? What are you waiting for? In addition to bonus content (great new stuff will be added regularly) you will always be in the loop - you'll never have to wonder when my newest release will hit the stores—AND you will get a free book as a special welcome gift.

Sign up now! http://freescifiromance.com

FIND YOUR INTERSTELLAR MATCH!

YOUR mate is out there. Take the test today and discover your perfect match. Are you ready for a sexy alien mate (or two)?

VOLUNTEER NOW!

interstellarbridesprogram.com

DO YOU LOVE AUDIOBOOKS?

Grace Goodwin's books are now available as
audiobooks...everywhere.

LET'S TALK!

Interested in joining my **Sci-Fi Squad**? Meet new like-minded sci-fi romance fanatics and chat with Grace! Be part of a private Facebook group that shares pictures and fun news! Join here:

https://www.facebook.com/groups/scifisquad/

Want to talk about Grace Goodwin books with others? Join the **SPOILER ROOM** and spoil away! Your GG BFFs are waiting! (And so is Grace) Join here:

https://www.facebook.com/groups/ggspoilerroom/

GET A FREE BOOK!

JOIN MY MAILING LIST TO BE THE FIRST TO KNOW OF NEW RELEASES, FREE BOOKS, SPECIAL PRICES AND OTHER AUTHOR GIVEAWAYS.

http://freescifiromance.com

ALSO BY GRACE GOODWIN

Chosen by the Vikens

Marked Mate

Interstellar Brides® Program Boxed Set - Books 6-8

Interstellar Brides® Program Boxed Set - Books 9-12

Interstellar Brides® Program Boxed Set - Books 13-16

Interstellar Brides® Program Boxed Set - Books 17-20

Interstellar Brides® Program Boxed Set - Books 21-24

Bad Boys of Rogue 5

Interstellar Brides® Program: The Colony

Surrender to the Cyborgs

Mated to the Cyborgs

Cyborg Seduction

Her Cyborg Beast

Cyborg Fever

Rogue Cyborg

Cyborg's Secret Baby

Her Cyborg Warriors

Claimed by the Cyborgs

The Colony Boxed Set 1

The Colony Boxed Set 2

The Colony Boxed Set 3

Interstellar Brides® Program: The Virgins

The Alien's Mate

His Virgin Mate

Claiming His Virgin

His Virgin Bride

His Virgin Princess

The Virgins - Complete Boxed Set

Interstellar Brides® Program: Ascension Saga

Ascension Saga, book 1

Ascension Saga, book 2

Ascension Saga, book 3

Trinity: Ascension Saga - Volume 1

Ascension Saga, book 4

Ascension Saga, book 5

Ascension Saga, book 6

Faith: Ascension Saga - Volume 2

Ascension Saga, book 7

Ascension Saga, book 8

Ascension Saga, book 9

Destiny: Ascension Saga - Volume 3

Interstellar Brides® Program: The Beasts

Bachelor Beast

Maid for the Beast

Beauty and the Beast

The Beasts Boxed Set - Books 1-3

Big Bad Beast

Beast Charming

Bargain with a Beast

The Beasts Boxed Set - Books 4-6

Beast's Secret Baby

SUBSCRIBE TODAY!

Hi there! Grace Goodwin here. I am SO excited to invite you into my intense, crazy, sexy, romantic, imagination and the worlds born as a result. From Battlegroup Karter to The Colony and on behalf of the entire Coalition Fleet of Planets, I welcome you! Visit my Patreon page for additional bonus content, sneak peaks, and insider information on upcoming books as well as the opportunity to receive NEW RELEASE BOOKS before anyone else! See you there! ~ Grace

Grace's PATREON: https://www.patreon.com/gracegoodwin

ABOUT GRACE

Grace Goodwin is a USA Today and international bestselling author of Sci-Fi and Paranormal romance with over a million books sold. Grace's titles are available worldwide on all retailers, in multiple languages, and in ebook, print, audio and other reading App formats.

Grace is a full-time writer whose earliest movie memories are of Luke Skywalker, Han Solo, and real, working light sabers. (Still waiting for Santa to come through on that one.) Now Grace writes sexy-as-hell sci-fi romance six days a week. In her spare time, she reads, watches campy sci-fi and enjoys spending time with family and friends. No matter where she is, there is always a part of her dreaming up new worlds and exciting characters for her next book.

Grace loves to chat with readers and can frequently be found lurking in her Facebook groups. Interested in joining her **Sci-Fi Squad**? Meet new like-minded sci-fi romance fanatics and chat with Grace! Join here: https://www.face book.com/groups/scifisquad/

Want to talk about Grace Goodwin books with others? Join the **SPOILER ROOM** and spoil away! Your GG BFFs are waiting! (And so is Grace) Join here:

https://www.facebook.com/groups/ggspoilerroom/

Printed in Great Britain
by Amazon